S0-EOG-634

The Zakhov Mission

ANDREI GULYASHKI

The Zakhov Mission

TRANSLATED BY MAURICE MICHAEL

1969

PUBLISHED FOR THE CRIME CLUB BY
DOUBLEDAY & COMPANY, INC.
GARDEN CITY, NEW YORK

Published in Bulgaria under the title
PRIKLOGYENIYEMA NA AVAKUM ZAKHOV
Jus Autor 1963

All of the characters in this book are fictitious,
and any resemblance to actual persons,
living or dead, is purely coincidental.

Library of Congress Catalog Card Number 69-21012
Translation copyright © 1968 by Cassell & Co., Ltd, 1968
All rights reserved
Printed in the United States of America
First edition in the United States of America

1

BRACKEN AND BRAMBLE cover the final slope that leads to the bald top of Karabair. Beyond it, to the south, the middle distance is corrugated with line upon line of wooded ridges, beyond which stretches a sunlit plain of intimidating vastness. The side of the highest of these wooded ridges bears a broad scar where it has been shorn of its trees and bushes by a broad, horizontal strip: the frontier. Beyond this shaven strip is the same mountain and above it is the same blue sky.

Yet it is a foreign country. So clear is the air here that from Karabair itself the frontier, even the sunlit distant plain, seem a mere stone's throw away, yet to reach either on foot would mean many hours of toil. This is not hospitable country. No smoke rises from the chimneys of homesteads; no sheep- or cow-bells tinkle about those wooded slopes. But eagles soar and wheel in the air above, and in the lacework of the shadows under the black pines deer move with delicate silent tread. In the arid valleys, the torrents off the mountainsides turn into meandering rivers with shallow beds that flood after sudden rain over stretches of marsh and reed-beds, the home of the spoonbill with its snow-white plumage. Sometimes a brown bear changing territory will ford a river and vanish into the green silence of the trees. This is a true no-man's land, a place where perhaps only wolves are really at home. In summer they hunt singly or in pairs; but once the snow has capped the crests of the trees with white, they band together in packs.

It was to these parts that the Thracian metal workers, samples of whose art you will see in the museums of Plovdiv and Sofia, came for their metals. Centuries later, when Marie Curie was working through her tons of pitchblende, a strange 'shooting party' had spent some time in the district. Now, you have only to mention the word 'Karabair' to the geologist and his eye will light up and he will sigh and wish he could get there.

North of Karabair the character of the country changes. Here it is rendered sombre by the dense forests that clothe the sides of the rounded hills, between which the valleys open and occasionally widen into a plain; but here again the signs of man are few, and the only houses to be seen are those of the village that lies tucked away at the foot of Karabair itself.

This is the village of Momchilovo, which, in the days of the Turks, went by the name of Ramadan-bey. It consists of three hundred houses, grouped in three hamlets set in a horseshoe between the two spurs running down from Karabair. Most of the houses are wooden, one-storeyed, with shingle roofs and bars across the narrow windows that face the road. On the other sides of the houses and in the courtyards, the windows are larger and their ledges bright with nasturtiums, honeysuckle and scarlet geraniums planted in jugs and pots.

Among the brick houses of the area known as 'Marco's Quarter' there is one of white stone, which used to belong to Ali Iliazov and is still known by his name, though it now houses the Geological Survey. It is a large house, almost a castle, built round a courtyard, and in fine weather you can see its tiled roof from the top of Karabair itself. Then there is the new school, a building of concrete and glass; the Co-operative Dairy with its rough-cast façade; and the huge, barrack-like buildings of the stables and cowhouses and sheep-pens of the Co-operative Farm. These are all new both in design and materials, and their modernity is in glaring contrast to the decrepitude of the other buildings in the village.

Viewed from above, from the mountainside, Momchilovo appears like a straggling tree-top nest of some large, untidy bird. Beyond it on all sides are the slopes of other hills and mountains, dotted, like the valleys between them, with pasture and outcrops of rocks. Through it all winds the ribbon of the road from Smolyan, now white in the gathering dusk. Within the horseshoe of the three hamlets is a scarred, humpy waste, scoured by torrential rains and covered with dense pine-thickets and scrub, the haunt of foxes. Out of this, and the darkness that covered it, there now appeared the tall figure of a man, walking easily along one of the paths that wound through the scrub. He appeared to be on familiar ground, for he was quite unconcerned by the sudden twists and turns of the path. He came from the north, stepping with the assurance of familiarity despite the darkness.

Black clouds were scudding past across the top of Karabair. The wind had got up and the air was now full of its sound. Occasionally a yellow flash of lightning lit up everything, to be followed after a long pause by the rumble of distant thunder. The man, however, seemed to be in no hurry; he even stopped once and lit a cigarette between his cupped hands, the red flicker of the flame wavering through the darkness.

The man reached the place where the path forked, the right arm straggling on to join the Smolyan road where it passed Marco's Quarter; the left-hand prong zigzagging between the hedges bounding the silent houses and emerging onto the slope that curled round the massive white stone structure of Iliazov's House. The top of the slope was almost level with the back wall of the courtyard and the man was accustomed to jump down here and take a short cut through the courtyard. He did this now. Pausing beneath a heavily barred window, he took two or three pulls at the cigarette he was smoking, then threw the stub on the ground and crushed it under his heel. He strode on towards the middle of the courtyard, where, midway between the door and the house itself, a great elm tree raised its tousled crest.

As the man drew level with the tree, a shadowy figure emerged and a voice croaked:

'Halt!'

The sentry held his rifle at the ready.

In the silence you could hear the thousand little voices of the tree, which was suddenly lit by a flash of lightning forking across the sky above Karabair. Recognizing the man, the sentry grounded his rifle and wagged his head reproachfully. The man smiled and ran his fingers through his wind-blown hair.

'Keep your eyes open,' he said to the sentry, and strode off into the darkness that quickly swallowed him up.

The sentry bowed his head wearily, twirled the end of his moustache, slung his rifle over his shoulder and began searching in his pockets for a cigarette.

The sky was overcast and the wind loud in the great elm, so that the sentry neither saw nor heard the figure that lightly rose up behind him. Pulling out a packet of cigarettes the sentry selected one, then suddenly he staggered, his knees sagged and he dropped to the ground like a log.

2

BY DAWN the storm had passed. The wind had swept all the clouds to the east and the sky above Karabair was clear and blue.

Sergeant-Major Georgi was walking up the road to the white stone house. He had held his head under the cold water of the fountain, but he still felt sleepy. He had had a bad night. The thunder had woken him and then he had started thinking all the unpleasant thoughts of those who have been too long away from home. He had not had any leave since he and Stoyan had been sent to Momchilovo as guards for the Geological Survey, and now more and more frequently he found himself imagining himself back in the fields at the foot of Marina-laka with maize reaching to his shoulders, or walking up to the door of his house and hearing across the fence the light footsteps of their neighbour's young daughter running barefoot across the dusty yard. It was not so bad for the other, he thought. Stoyan was over forty and a widower. His only child, a son, was grown up, and studying at the Technical College. But he, Georgi, was not yet thirty and the thought of the maize fields scorching in the sun and the brown legs and bare feet of the girl next door was apt to quicken his pulse.

Peevish and sleepy, he trudged on up the slope, his cap pushed back off his forehead. Darkness had fled and round about in the homesteads ducks were quacking and cocks crowing. Turning right at the fork, he walked on towards the white house and, reaching it, walked in through the gate which was standing wide open as usual. He gave the accustomed whistle, which normally brought the gentle, patient Stoyan up at a run, even after a night's sentry-go. They would then smoke a cigarette together, saying little, before Stoyan went off to bed and Georgi began his far from onerous duties.

Georgi repeated his whistle. There was no reply. He looked round. All was peaceful. Silence reigned. Even the foliage of the great elm was still and quiet. Then, suddenly, he caught sight of a cap lying on the ground, a service cap. There was nothing really so extraordinary about that, yet at the sight of it his legs began to tremble, as if he had just climbed all the way to the top of Karabair. It struck him that, not possessing a watch, he ought to look east and see how near to sunrise it was, so as to have an idea of the time, but he could not take his eyes off the cap. Feeling horribly anxious he began walking towards it. Two paces and then he saw him. He was lying on his back on the ground with his arms outstretched, in the relaxed attitude shepherds adopt when sleeping out on warm summer nights. It was thus that Stoyan often slept.

Could he have fallen asleep at his post? Even though there was nothing doing in such a place, the very idea was incredible. Georgi took another step forward, then halted again, one foot raised, gaping.

Stoyan's head was enveloped in a piece of lemon yellow turkish towelling, so that neither hair, ears nor jaws were visible. More sinister, perhaps, was the position of the rifle. It was lying obliquely under him with his left shoulder resting on the barrel and the butt almost parallel with his right elbow.

The figure on the ground never moved. It looked dead.

Trembling, Georgi squatted down beside the body and quickly unwound the towel from its head. As he undid the knot in which it was tied at the back, his fingers became covered with blood, sticky but still warm.

The towelling gave off a pungent smell and Georgi flung it

to one side and stared in horror at the other's livid face and blue closed eyelids. He shuddered, put his hand under the man's head and raised it up. It weighed like lead. Dead!

He undid the buttons of Stoyan's tunic and put his ear to his vest. No, he could hear a heart-beat, faint but unmistakable. He got to his feet, hesitated a moment, then set off at a run back the way he had come.

3

ONE DAY I shall kill that cock, the vet thought. It was his landlord's cock and had lost most of the feathers on its neck, which at that moment he would dearly have liked to wring, for once again the ghastly bird had flown up onto the sill of his window, flapped its wings noisily and then shrieked out a series of the most raucous cock-a-doodle-doos in greeting to a day that for anyone else was still far from beginning. The young vet turned over, pulled the covers over his ear and tried to get to sleep again. Just as he felt himself sinking into slumber, there was a great banging on his window and a loud voice cried 'Wake up, wake up! You're wanted.'

This time, however, it was not an animal that required his services, but a human being. The young vet listened to the Sergeant-Major's rather garbled story with growing apprehension. Normally his responsibilities to the Survey were confined to their two pack mules, but, as it would be some considerable time before the doctor could arrive, he thought that he ought to have a look and see what he could do.

Fortunately he had among his things a medical syringe, a

packet of hypodermic needles and some ampoules of camphorated oil and these he shoved into his pocket. Then he set off at a brisk pace with the Sergeant-Major.

The earthen colour of his patient's eyelids terrified him. Why one should be more acutely aware of one's responsibility when giving a person an injection than when administering one to an animal, he did not know, but he almost dropped the syringe he had got ready, then just thrust it in and gave the injection without first feeling the man's pulse, as he at once realized he ought to have done. Then he helped Georgi get the heavy, limp bundle onto his back, picked up the man's rifle and cap and the bloodstained towel which smelt strongly of chloroform, and walked on after the Sergeant-Major. They decided to take the wounded man to the vet's room in the Spiridons' house, which was much nearer than the victim's own lodgings.

Together they got him onto the vet's bed and, while Georgi went off to make his report, there being no telephone in these villagers' houses, the vet washed his hands in surgical spirit and examined the wound. As far as he could ascertain, the skull was not fractured. There were several abrasions running from the crown to the base of the neck, but there had been no great loss of blood. It looked as though unconsciousness was due to the chloroform rather than to the severity of the blow the man had received. The nasty brick colour of his face, especially round his mouth and nose, was also due to the chloroform, or so the vet supposed, and he wondered just what quantity the poor wretch had absorbed. Too much? He knew how much his own good animals could stand, but not humans. They weren't really his line at all. On the whole he did not like them, and this little incident brought home to him the fact that he could never have been a doctor. Anyway the man's pulse was obviously getting stronger, so he had no real fears about his state, especially when he noticed that the eyes were losing their cadaverous colour and little beads of perspiration were appearing on the man's upper lip.

Reassured, he lit his spirit lamp—Momchilovo had not yet received the blessings of electric power—and began making coffee. The water had not boiled when his room was invaded by the local dignitaries—breathless from running, perturbed and excited by the news of what had happened and determined not to be left out of anything. The first arrival was the president of the Agricultural Co-operative, who thus stole a march on the head of the Geological Survey, the injured man's titular C.O. He arrived a couple of minutes later and hard on his heels came the assistant geologist. The Sergeant-Major, reassured as to the man's condition, went and stood guard outside the door.

'How bad is he?' asked old Grozdan, president of the Agricultural Co-operative, as he leaned against the wall, his eyes alight with the thrill and excitement misfortune brings when it overtakes others.

'I don't think he's bad at all,' the young vet said. 'Unless there's concussion, which I don't believe, he'll recover consciousness quite soon.'

No one else spoke. Colonel Injov, C.O. of the Survey, looked at his watch.

'It's nearly five o'clock now. Dr Nacheva should be here soon,' he said.

The young vet could just imagine how Dr Nacheva's eyes would blaze with professional jealousy when she saw that he, the vet, had been giving first aid, and he rather shrank at the prospect. He was rather attracted by Nadia Nacheva, intimidating though she could be.

'Lakité's a good eight miles away,' someone observed, 'and you can't walk it in less than two hours.'

'I said that she will be here soon, and she will,' Colonel

Injov said icily. Then he put his head out of the window and spoke to Georgi.

'Have you arranged for a guard on the White House?'

The reply was apparently affirmative, for the Colonel then turned back to those in the room and deigned to explain.

'I sent the Co-operative Farm's lorry for Dr Nacheva, so it won't take her much over a quarter of an hour to get here.'

At that moment the water for the vet's coffee came to the boil, and as he took it off the flame he heard old Grozdan ask, 'Have you checked to see if anything's been stolen?'

'That's for the police,' the Colonel replied in an irritable tone. 'I've made a preliminary examination, of course.' Then, almost as though speaking to himself, he went on, 'One pane of glass broken, a cupboard forced open, two thousand leva missing—and a sketch map,' he added in a whisper.

'A map!' Grozdan exclaimed, eyes popping out of his head.

The Colonel's jaw set, as if he regretted saying what he had.

The vet took the wounded man's pulse once more—that looked professional and efficient—and was gratified to feel how much stronger it was. He had no doubt now that he would come round quite soon.

He made the coffee, poured some into a little cup and sat down beside the wounded man. As he placed his hand on the man's forehead the lids fluttered, but the eyes were still unseeing. The vet spoke his name and gave his shoulder a gentle shake. He sighed deeply.

'Can you hear me?' the vet asked.

His lips moved.

'All's well,' the vet said and looked round at the others, smiling.

The Colonel sighed with relief, put his hand to his pocket and pulled out a toffee. He unwrapped it, popped it into his mouth and folded up the paper. For some weeks he had been trying to smoke less and that made him consume a vast quantity of sweets.

The vet put an extra pillow under Stoyan's head and held the cup of coffee to his lips, but he did not seem to realize what was intended, for he remained as he was, stretched out, his face motionless, eyelids lowered, as if not hearing what was said to him.

At that moment the Spiridons' scrawny-necked cock flapped its wings and uttered such a piercing crow that they all shuddered and the wounded man opened his eyes, which had suddenly become clear and comprehending. He looked at them all for a moment, an expression of mounting astonishment on his face, then he suddenly frowned and gave vent to a deep, melancholy sigh. He then took several sips of coffee, wiped his lips with the back of his hand and let his head fall back onto the pillow. He lay thus, his eyes open and apparently fixed on old Grozdan. His gaze appeared to agitate the old farmer, who shuffled his feet and seemed not to know what to do with his hands.

'What happened, Stoyan?' Grozdan asked in a voice that lacked its usual gruffness.

They all turned and looked at the wounded man, waiting in silent expectation for him to speak.

Stoyan wrinkled his brow.

'It happened so quickly,' he said and moistened his blue lips with his tongue. 'He had said goodnight and walked on and I was lighting a cigarette and he must have come back without me realizing it . . . and who could have heard anything, the way the wind was blowing in the old tree?'

So, between sips of coffee and continual promptings, Stoyan told us his story, the only other character in which was Momchilovo's schoolmaster, Metodi Parashkevov, upon whom everyone tended to look as a paragon of all the virtues.

Metodi Parashkevov often went shooting in the wilderness

to the east of the Zmeitza, from which his best way back led across the courtyard of Iliazov's big white house; or rather, that was a short cut to the house of Mrs Anna Balabanova, with whom he lodged. The schoolmaster was a good shot and seldom returned empty-handed. Thanks to his straight eye, Anna Balabanova had a rabbitskin waistcoat and a coat of fox-fur. He was not a man you could easily get to stand you a drink, but he was generous with the game he shot and seldom kept anything for himself. On his way home, he always stopped to exchange a few words with the sentry at the Survey. Despite his education, he was not in the least affected and was always ready to chat, especially about animals, the wily ways of the fox and the moods of wolf and bear. On the evening in question, however, the schoolmaster had been without his gun. It had been late when he got back. In fact the Great Bear was already turning towards the Danube. Lightning was playing about the sky above Karabair and thunder rumbling round the mountains farther south. What had struck Stoyan as unusual was the fact that Parashkevov had been in a hurry, seemingly as anxious to get home as if he had had a wife and children waiting for him, instead of just an empty room. He had scarcely said good evening before he was hurrying on and it was while Stoyan, wondering at the schoolmaster's unaccustomed brusqueness, was lighting a cigarette from the packet in his pocket, that something had hit him on the back of the head and he had known no more until he had come to and found himself in bed in the vet's room.

There was a moment's silence when Stoyan finished, and they all looked at each other. Then the Colonel made a gesture, as though brushing a fly from his face, and said, 'Come, Stoyan; are you sure it was the schoolmaster who hit you? Couldn't there have been someone else hiding there?'

Stoyan frowned.

'The courtyard, as you know, sir, is absolutely empty. There is that tree in the middle and that's all. I was standing under the tree as the schoolmaster came striding down the hill. There was no one else.'

'All right. But couldn't your assailant have been hidden behind the gate? He could have come out the moment the schoolmaster walked on and struck you down—couldn't he?'

'Of course,' Grozdan put in. 'Perfectly possible.'

Stoyan sighed and closed his eyes.

'No, he couldn't, sir,' he said at length. 'The distance from the gate to the tree is such that while someone was covering it at a run I would have had time to fish out a cigarette and light it and even take a pull or two, but I had only just got my hand into my pocket—had hardly got hold of a cigarette.'

He said no more.

Colonel Injov drew himself up, tugged his tunic into place, sighed and, going to the window, ordered Georgi to go and arrest the schoolmaster and put seals on the door of his room.

'You're to tell the owners of the house that they will be held responsible if anyone enters that room before the examining magistrate arrives,' he said.

Georgi saluted, turned and marched briskly away, startling the scrawny-necked cock, which gave a raucous squawk of fright and irritation.

As the vet took hold of Stoyan's wrist to take his pulse, they heard a lorry pull up outside. The doctor had arrived.

Dr Nacheva was attractive, even when, as now, her pretty little nose caught the smell of chloroform, her eyes flashed angrily with professional jealousy and shot daggers at the young vet who stood there looking rather sheepish.

'Chloroform,' she said. 'Have *you* been trying your hand at surgery?' There was a hint of menace in her voice that went better with the angry look in her eyes than with her honeyed tone. It touched the vet on the raw, however, and he was on the point of telling her that he knew his place and limitations and that there was no need for her to get on her high horse, but he bit back the words. You could not be angry with someone as pretty as Dr Nacheva.

'Stoyan's assailant administered the anaesthetic, not I,' he said and pointed to the yellow towel.

4

THE LIGHT from the reading-lamp was almost lost in the growing daylight that poured into the room from a large open window. That the room was occupied by a bachelor was evident from the masculine severity of its furnishings and the many books that were stacked on the floor or ranged untidily on the shelves that lined the walls. On the narrow single bed lay the figure of a man, sound asleep. But the bedclothes were untidy and the reading-lamp by the bed still alight, so the occupant of the bed had evidently found sleep slow in coming and had lain there reading. He had in fact read until daybreak.

He was a man of about forty, nearly six feet tall, with broad shoulders and a barely noticeable stoop. He had a long, rather thin face, with a high forehead, prominent cheekbones and a good square jaw. His eyes were blue and usually calm and pensive but they could also be unexpectedly—except to certain types of women—gay and roguish. His fingers were long and sensitive.

This Avakum Zakhov was something of an enigma, not only to his landlady, but to many of his acquaintances. He was a man of many parts. He had taken a degree in history at the University of Sofia; published a paper on epigraphy. Then he had gone to Moscow and taken a postgraduate course in archaeology, specializing in the preservation and restoration of archaeological objects. On his return from Moscow he had taken a job in the Institute of Archaeology in Sofia, where he was soon put in charge of the restoration work; while doing this he yet found time to take a correspondence course in science at the Technological College and had attended evening classes in photography. It was then that certain events, which do not concern this story, introduced Zakhov into the service of the State in another capacity: that of counter-espionage agent.

Zakhov was a light sleeper, and the telephone beside his bed had not rung more than twice before he had stretched out a hand and calmly removed the receiver. Now he was listening to a voice telling him that a service car was on its way to fetch him. The head of his department wished to see him.

And then Zakhov remembered that officially he was on leave —as from that morning.

5

Colonel Manov had a big office into which the early sunlight was flooding as Zakhov was shown in. The hands of the electric clock pointed to seven o'clock.

'Sorry to have to send for you on the first day of your leave, Zakhov,' he said with a friendly look. 'I hope the summons wasn't too unpleasant a surprise?'

'I'm all in favour of surprises, Colonel,' Zakhov said easily.

'Even disagreeable ones?'

Zakhov smiled.

'According to this report,' Colonel Manov said, tapping the papers on the desk in front of him, 'since 10 August a secret transmitter, working on ultra-short waves in the area round the Karabair massif, has on three occasions transmitted coded messages and received replies. As you know the country is geologically very interesting and potentially valuable. There have been reports that leninite can be found there and we have a survey team in the field there now. It is an area of top security, because others may suspect its possibilities as, indeed, they seem to do. The position of the transmitter appears to be somewhere within twenty miles north or south of the Karabair massif. This is difficult country, especially if you want to traverse it at night. The first transmission, at any rate the first that the monitoring section heard, was on the night of 10–11 August. It began at 2200 hours. The text of the message is short but coded; both the transmitter and the answering station changed wavelength twice during the fifteen minutes they were transmitting. Measures were taken at once to seal off the area and it has since been searched but without result. This is not surprising, as even with helicopters it would take weeks to search it properly.

'On 19 August there was another transmission, again at 2200. There were guards actually on the mountain at the time but this time the detectors gave the position of the transmitter as behind them, a mile or so to the east of the village of Momchilovo. This is a district known locally as the Zmeitza, an area of very rough, broken country where, I am told, the devil himself would be unable to find you, if you wished to hide from him. Apparently this was a rather peculiar transmission consisting only of a few coded phrases, then a succession of sounds. All very mysterious.

'Unfortunately, we still haven't managed to decode the messages. We have probably missed a word or two when the wavelengths changed and that has not made the cipher people's job any easier. Also, we may well be dealing with a foreign language.

'Now comes a report of disquieting happenings in the village of Momchilovo itself. Last night one of the windows in a building occupied by the Geological Survey—the one I mentioned—was forced, a top secret plan and a largish sum of money taken. The guard was hit on the head and chloroformed, for which dire deed the local schoolmaster has been arrested.'

Here the Colonel cocked an eye on Zakhov, who smiled in response.

'Mysterious signals, chloroform, a secret plan stolen,' he said. 'This is a thriller.'

'I know,' said the Colonel. 'It does not perhaps sound the sort of things to recall a man from leave for—you are on leave, aren't you?'

'I was,' Zakhov said with the faintest note of bitterness in his voice. 'All booked to go to the Black Sea.' He sighed.

'You can still go, if you want to. Captain Kovachev has taken charge locally for the time being. He could, at a pinch, see the thing through.'

'All right, all right,' said Zakhov. 'I'm volunteering. Forget my leave. It can wait. I shall lie in the sun some other time—I hope!' he added. 'Is there anything more to tell me?'

'Merely that Momchilovo and the surrounding areas are being patrolled by men of the Frontier Security. All roads are guarded and watched. Captain Kovachev is at Plovdiv, but going to Momchilovo. In view of the importance of this area and the possible nature of the messages, this transmitter and those who work it simply have to be found. Hence your recall.'

'I suppose you wish me to start at Momchilovo?'

'Please.'

'Good. Then the sooner the better. Can I have transport?'

'Of course. But in view of the roads in those parts, if you

21

can call them that, you had better take a motorcycle rather than a car.'

'So, it's goodbye to comfort. Never mind!' Zakhov smiled and got to his feet. 'No doubt the trip will be good for my liver.'

History and archaeology may have been the real loves of Avakum Zakhov, but he was human for all that. Indeed, he was an incurable romantic always searching for the girl of his dreams, despite the fact that twenty years of testing possible candidates had not yet produced one that was entirely satisfactory. The latest candidate was a certain young lady by the name of Sia Zheinova, who had some sort of chemical degree and worked in a big laboratory, making nothing more epoch-making than cosmetics. She was twenty-two and when Zakhov first met her had confessed to a passion for basketball. However, she had showed a lively and intelligent interest in archaeology and proved a most congenial companion. So congenial, in fact, that Zakhov had proposed that she take her holiday at the same time as he his leave and that they should make a trip together up the Ropotamo. He would fish and collect the wood for their camp fire and she should cook the catch, and together they would listen to the cries of the night birds and . . . and . . . Zakhov's heart was full of hope and joyful anticipation. After some days of this life, they would go on to Madara, he had told her, to see the famous Horseman of Madara, a wonderful monument to the glories of the ancient kingdom of Bulgaria. Madara also has an ancient amphitheatre with great rocks covered with ivy and red lichen and protected by a sort of open stone roof. He had been looking forward to explaining to Sia the mechanism of the optical illusion caused by that vast heap of polished stones, where you only need to walk twenty paces away and to your companion you will look no bigger than a ninepin.

Indeed, Zakhov had planned a holiday very much to his taste. From Madara they were to have gone on to Preslav to visit the ruins of Aboba and Pliska, where earlier he had been on a dig. Then they would go on to Tirnovo, where he would revel in nostalgic memories of his youth and end up on the sunny, sandy shores of the Black Sea. It was a delightful trip he had planned, and one well calculated to test the genuineness of Sia's interest in archaeology and archaeologists.

It now looked very much as if those delights would have to be postponed. Sia did not get her holiday for another week; but it scarcely seemed as if this mission could be satisfactorily concluded in the time. Not wishing to burn his boats, however, Zakhov merely sent her a note saying that the Museum had asked him to do something for them that involved going away for a couple of days. Then he packed a bag, mounted his motorcycle and rode off.

6

BEING of a romantic disposition, Zakhov had an incurable love of disguise and never missed an opportunity to indulge it. Thus when he came to the gorge of Momin Prohod, where the road and its companion the River Maritza plunge through a defile, he stopped, wheeled his motorcycle off the road and looked round for a suitable 'dressing-room'. In that wilderness of bushes and boulders there were plenty to choose from and soon Avakum Zakhov was squatted behind a bush from which hung a little mirror, busy changing his appearance. Zakhov was too intelligent not to realize that this was quite unnecessary, but there was still enough of the boy in him for him to delight in 'dressing up'—and who, today, will blame him?

Ten minutes later a man with a slightly hunched back, a left shoulder that was higher than the right, a thin, drooping horseshoe moustache and a striking livid scar that ran from just above his left eye across his sunburned cheek, came walking out of the bushes towards the road. He wore an old leather jerkin, a cap pulled well down over his brow, and might have been a mechanic on his way to restore some car or tractor to life. He wheeled Zakhov's motorcycle to the road, seated himself in the saddle, started up with a deft kick and rode off. The road out of the gorge was a series of hairpin bends that had to be treated with respect, but once out of the defile he was in among the last spurs of the foothills. There the corners were reasonably gentle and the surface good, and he was able to speed up to a steady seventy, almost as if he was already on the great central plain which, farther on, stretched ahead of him for nearly two hundred miles, all the way to the Black Sea and the golden sands where he and Sia were *not* going to lie side by side.

Soon he was riding beside the waters of the great artificial lake and reservoir, where the astonished Western tourists always came to gape in the summer, as if no Communist country had ever built an irrigation system. Zakhov smiled. How naïve they were, he said to himself; . . . then he laughed aloud, remembering that a short while before he had been squatting behind a bush engaged in the schoolboy's occupation of disguising himself. Away out on the lake was a white yacht, looking grey in the shadow of the one cloud in the blue sky. A fish rose close to the shore and Zakhov told himself that he and Sia could spend a very happy holiday there without going all the way to the Black Sea. The pine trees that lined part of the shore would provide an excellent camping place.

He sighed, because he knew in his heart of hearts that whatever the next few weeks might hold in store for him, it was not the arms of young Sia and the grilled trout that he himself had caught.

A mile or two before the junction where the road he must take to reach Momchilovo led off to the south, Zakhov caught signt of another motorcycle in front of him and thought that he recognized the crouched figure of Captain Kovachev. Zakhov accelerated, so did the machine in front. Faster and faster they went, Zakhov blew his horn, but the noise the two machines were making, doubled and redoubled by the boulder-strewn side of a spur that at that point ran parallel with the road, was such that it was scarcely possible that this message would reach the figure in front.

Taking advantage of a straight stretch, Zakhov turned his accelerator right over, roared past the other machine and braked to a stop some hundred yards ahead of it. Zakhov leaped off and turned, saw the man on the other machine dismount and thrust his right hand into an inside pocket on the left of his tunic. There they stood facing each other. Zakhov lit a cigarette and looked round him: a steep slope covered with rocks and pine trees and spruce, fern and bushes, towered up over his head. Below, farther down the slope out of which the road at that point had been cut, the ground was riven with clefts and ravines filled with green treetops so closely crowded that the sun could never reach the ground out of which they grew. This was a place of aged trees that must have witnessed much of the country's history in the making. Perhaps they had sheltered the survivors of Benkovski's men after the fall of Bratzigovo. Or had the Turks caught them all before they got there? Turks? To whom had those secret messages been sent? The thought reminded Zakhov of his mission and looking at the figure of this man, whom he now knew was Kovachev, still holding his hand inside his tunic, Zakhov smiled. It pleased him to know that his disguise had deceived the other, not that he considered Kovachev particularly bright, but even so . . .

There was a moment of absolute silence while the men looked at each other and Zakhov thought: 'He's got his finger on the trigger.' Then he waved his hand gaily, called, 'Hallo, Kovachev! How are you?' and strode towards him.

Recognizing the voice, Kovachev withdrew his hand from his inside pocket where he kept his revolver and again seated himself astride his motorcycle.

'At it again, I see,' he said. 'I can't understand why you always want to make up, as if you were a ruddy actor going on the set. Who on earth do you think it impresses? It's too childish. And that scar. Pretty unobtrusive! Just the thing for a spy wanting to pass unnoticed!'

Zakhov laughed.

'But it amuses me,' he said, 'and not much else in this job does. Besides, you never know when it might pay dividends. Let me have my little foible.'

Captain Kovachev put his foot on the kick-starter.

'Ever been to Momchilovo before?' he asked, as his engine sprang to life. 'No? Then you'd better follow me. And after we turn off, keep your eyes open for potholes and stones. The road's ghastly.'

Some five minutes later they reached the fork, beyond which the white ribbon of the main road led on down the shoulder of the last mountain and wound lower and lower through the dark green of the wooded foothills, disappearing temporarily behind a blue fold in the ground. Then it reappeared, much narrower and less sharply defined, out on the flat plain across which it spread like a vapour trail, till it was swallowed up in the blue of the distance, half-way to the sand dunes that fringed the Black Sea. For a moment Zakhov thought again of Sia and the holiday he was not going to have, then he turned down the other road, an unmetalled dirt road. The jolts of the first few yards convinced him that what Kovachev had said about it was less than the truth. But whatever the surface, the setting was lovely. The road dived steeply down the side of a wooded bowl scooped out of the side of the mountain. Its flat greensward, through which bounded a stream, was crossed at one point by a wooden footbridge, the only sign of human habitation, for though he looked everywhere among the trees he could not see a roof, not even the slanting tip of a crane at a well. Beyond the bowl the road dived again, though not so steeply, down a southern slope on which the trees were beginning to thin out. A snake moved across the path and Zakhov thought it looked very like the small Turkish boa he had recently read about in a nature article. There was something interesting about it, but he couldn't remember what. The boa slipped in under a low bush, the leaves of which had provided the model of the pattern on many of the ancient pots he had dug up. But the road was so bad and the jolts so violent that Zakhov was unable to think of archaeology or anything else; he just had to concentrate all his attention on steering and keeping his seat. Then a bend in the road opened up an idyllic scene, with a little house on an eminence beside the stream and the crouched figure of a smiling child pausing in the act of filling a pan at the water to look up at the exciting disturbance. The road dived into a green tunnel, from which the overhanging trees shut out the sun, and the rocky walls, covered with red lichen, echoed and re-echoed the splutter of the two exhausts till it sounded like the rattle of rifle fire. Emerging into the sunlight again, the road flattened out and led across a parched, boulder-strewn expanse where what little grass there was seemed to have been nibbled away by goats, the signs of whose passage were everywhere. This was an escarpment that dropped not too steeply down to a sunlit plain below. As they reached the edge, from where the road zigzagged down, Kovachev pulled up and, when Zakhov joined him, pointed to three clusters of houses just visible over the rim of the escarpment, and said, 'Momchilovo.' Beyond, on the other side of the valley floor which had not yet widened out, was the wooded slope of a mountainside.

'Karabair,' Kovachev said, then his arm swung round till it pointed left, to the east, and there, on the far side of the village and a mile or more beyond it, Zakhov saw a vision of chaos. An area of several square miles, it must have been, of hills, bumps and hillocks, all bare and arid, mostly rock, torn and riven with deep crevasses and defiles; jagged ridges ended in sharp needle tips, others brandished great cudgels of brown stone above their rounded backs. Some the wind had carved into a tracery that at that distance looked almost lace-like and delicate. Even in the sunlight that bathed it, it now looked the very home of nature's violence, a cruel place about which there was something unhealthy because some of the deeper ravines, which the afternoon sun did not penetrate, seemed to be filled with white vapour, conjuring up thoughts of miasmas and werewolves. Zakhov shuddered and could not repress the hope that he would not have to go there at night.

'That's the Zmeitza,' Kovachev said. 'I've not been there yet and I'm not all that keen to visit it, though I suppose we shall have to. The people here have some nasty tales to tell about it. Apparently it's not so bare as it looks from here. There are bushes in the ravines and a few little valleys hidden away here and there, so there's plenty of cover and, apparently, plenty of wolves and foxes in it, if nothing else. There's no road, not even a path, except an animal track or two, and they say that some of the ravines are deep enough to be crevasses; the temperature at the bottom is noticeably higher than up above and either there are hot springs or some other sources of damp, because vapour always seems to be rising from some of them. God help us if we have to search all that for this transmitter.

You'd need a couple of helicopters and then you wouldn't see half.'

For a moment they sat astride their cycles gazing in silence at the Zmeitza. If this had been the target at which Zeus had practised throwing his thunderbolts, it could scarcely have been more chaotic, Zakhov thought.

'Pretty nasty,' he said, compelled to understatement by the feeling that all adjectives were inadequate.

'But worse in winter,' Kovachev went on. 'Apparently this is the local sanctuary for wolves, and a couple of years ago, in that hard winter, a small pack of them killed and ate the local game warden. That year, they say, the brutes kept a regular watch on the road between Lakité and Momchilovo, like a lot of highwaymen. No one dared go anywhere on foot, even in daylight.'

'If the signals came from there,' Zakhov said, 'they would have had to be carefully aimed, because the range of a portable transmitter, which must have been used, would be tiny. Unless . . .' he broke off, but made a mental note to ask whether any aircraft had been heard over the area during the nights in question.

'It was on the fringe of the Zmeitza, over there,' Kovachev went on, 'that that foreign agent was caught last October. Kademov—wasn't that his name?'

Zakhov did not reply.

'Yes, Kademov it was. He was a native of Lakité, a village which you can't see from here, but it's over the ridge there. You can see a bit of the road to it circling that bluff.'

A shadow flitted across the ground just in front of his motor-cycle and, looking up, Zakhov saw the spread, motionless wings of a bearded eagle gliding majestically no more than a hundred feet above him. A glimpse of its cruel eyes and beak and it was past. That's what you need to be, if you're to search this place,

Zakhov thought. And if I was a quail or a pheasant, I'd try to keep well away from that beak.

Then the two men started up their engines again and rode down the zigzag road that led to the valley floor and the village of Momchilovo.

7

COLONEL MANOV was puzzled. On the desk in front of him he had the reports of the two men he had sent to Momchilovo, reports that reached exactly opposite conclusions. Why had he sent two men? Because he knew that Kovachev was a pedestrian and painstaking investigator, who yet lacked the intellectual flexibility necessary to see far beyond his own nose; while Zakhov, with his academic training and romantic disposition, was inclined to be too clever and overlook the obvious, just because it was too obvious. He had hoped that the two reports would agree, in which case he could have felt quite sure. But now! You would hardly think the men were on the same job.

The reports were concerned in the first instance with the attack on the sentry at the Geological Survey in Momchilovo and the theft of the secret document, of which the local schoolmaster, Metodi Parashkevov, was suspected and held in custody. Of him, Captain Kovachev wrote:

> He is forty-five and a bachelor. He looks like a true highlander and is tanned and weatherbeaten like one who lives largely out of doors both in summer and winter. Locally, he is said to be a very keen and excellent shot.

He was born at Preslav. His parents were people of means, comfortably off. They owned a large vineyard. His father died in 1945 and his mother a year later. He has no brothers or sisters. He has held teaching posts under the old régime at Kolarovgrad and at Provadia. Between the beginning of the new régime on 9 September 1944 and the end of 1946 he lived in Sofia, but appears not to have had a job (?). Then, early in 1947, he applied *of his own free will* for a teaching post in the most desolate part of the Rhodopes (!).

The people of Momchilovo have a good opinion of him, but I cannot help feeling that he is an astute and dangerous enemy. There is every reason to suppose that while living in Sofia he was recruited by a foreign intelligence service and then got himself sent to the Rhodopes, near the frontier. To facilitate contact with agents and others crossing the frontier illegally, he has affected a passion for climbing and walking in the mountains and for shooting. He has thus been able to come and go as he wished, having clandestine meetings with secret agents, saboteurs and other traitors in secret places.

The charges preferred against him—theft of a secret document from the Geological Survey and assaulting a sentry— would appear to be incontestable. The sentry was hit on the head with a revolver less than thirty seconds after talking with him. The towel, impregnated with chloroform, belonged to him, as is borne out by his landlady and neighbours. In a drawer in his room we found a large bottle of chloroform, equipped with a siphon mechanism, partly empty. Beneath the broken window in the H.Q. of the Geological Survey we found a Bouzloudja cigarette stub, which is the kind that he normally smokes. In the pocket of his coat was a packet of Bouzloudja containing seven cigarettes. When arrested he was packing his rucksack. . . . His arrest seems to have taken him by surprise and this would account for his not having hidden or got rid of the bottle of chloroform.

There are a number of witnesses to the fact that latterly he has frequently returned home about midnight (!).

His attitude during interrogation has been one of complete assurance, combined with a pretence at indignation and shock that he should be suspected.

When asked: *What were you doing up to midnight, when you talked to the sentry?* he replied: *I went for a walk in the vicinity of the village.* I then asked: *Where exactly?* He replied: *To the west.* Yet a witness, Marco Krumov, who lives on the eastern fringe of the villlage, swears to having seen him about ten o'clock that evening on the road that leads from Monchilovo to Lakité at the point where it runs close to the Zmeitza. Now the Zmeitza, which is where the agent Kademov was caught last October, lies to the east of the village.

When asked: *How is it that your towel was found round Stoyan's head?* he replied: *Do you really think that's the only towel of its kind in Bulgaria?* I then asked him: *Where do you normally hang your towel?* He replied: *Just outside the kitchen. On the coatstand in the hall.* We made an exhaustive search of the hall and also of his room, but were unable to find a towel.

When asked to explain why he had chloroform in his possession, he said: *I am carrying out some research in Natural History and I use it on occasion when experimenting on animals and insects.* (N.B., Metodi Parashkevov read chemistry and geology at Sofia University.)

Considering the strangeness of a man of his ability holding such a minor position, the circumstances in which the sentry was attacked and wounded, the lack of sincerity of the replies of the accused during interrogation, I am firmly of the opinion that he was the author of the attack and we are here faced with a case of deliberate, organized espionage. What remains to be done is to discover what accomplices he has and who they are.

This report is accompanied by the following:
- (*a*) 1 towel (Turkish towelling);
- (*b*) 1 cigarette stub, Bouzloudja;
- (*c*) 1 packet of Bouzloudja containing 7 cigarettes;
- (*d*) 1 syphon of chloroform;
- (*e*) 5 pieces of glass from the broken pane in the window of the Geological Survey.

Pinned to the report was another piece of paper on which was typed:

We have examined the pieces of glass as requested. Two of them carry thumbprints indentical in every way with those of Metodi Parashkevov. Parashkevov must have touched these pieces of glass.

We have similarly examined the cigarette stub sent to us for fingerprints. These are not as distinct as might have been wished, but they are sufficiently similar to the prints of the right thumb of Metodi Parashkevov for us to be able to say that it is quite probable they are identical. We would say that there is a sixty-per-cent probability that Metodi Parashkevov smoked this cigarette before it was thrown away.

Beside the folder was yet another piece of paper which the Colonel now picked up and read again.

The stub of Bouzloudja cigarette sent to us for examination had been slightly flattened on one side of the upper end by a narrow metal object with two edges. The marks are consistent with those that would be made by a heel or toe with an iron tip.

Slowly the Colonel picked up the receiver of his telephone and asked for the governor of Smolyan gaol, where Metodi

Parashkevov was being held in custody. A brief conversation, a wait of ten minutes, then a voice at the end of the line told him that Metodi Parashkevov was in fact wearing shoes the toes and heels of which were tipped with iron.

There was so much circumstantial evidence that it looked as if Captain Kovachev was correct in his conclusion. Of course, the stolen map had not been found either on the schoolmaster or in the rucksack he had been found packing. What had happened to it? Had he had time to send it on its way? A feeling of doubt returned and the Colonel picked up the report of his second officer, Avakum Zakhov, in whom he had always placed more confidence than in Slavi Kovachev. Zakhov seemed to attach little or no importance to this circumstantial evidence. Why? Just intuition—which had proved itself right now on more than one occasion? Logic? Or had he more to go on than he had put in his report. Skipping the usual service preamble the Colonel began to read again.

> I always start by suspecting two people—the most obvious and the least likely—but I must say straightaway that I have a number of reservations to make concerning Metodi Parashkevov, on whom suspicion seems to rest at the moment. I do not at this juncture say that he is innocent; I do not give him a necessarily clean bill, but there is something about him that tells me that there is no evil in him, that such a man cannot be a criminal. True, there is considerable evidence against him, but it is all circumstantial: the brief conversation with the sentry; the towel; possession of chloroform; a cigarette stub that could have been thrown down by him—he is a suspect, if no more. And yet the method of attack, the whole way in which the crime has been committed, especially the forcing of the windows etc. at the Geological Survey, has so much about it that is puzzling, even contradictory, that it would seem to indicate

that Metodi Parashkevov is not, or may not be, guilty of it. I shall elaborate on this on my return, when I can report to you verbally.

In the short time available, I have obtained the following basic facts about him which would seem rather to confirm the above opinion, than otherwise.

His parents were quite well-to-do. Both are now dead. Nothing he has done either before 9 September or since entitles us to assume that he has ever held reactionary views. He used the years when he was not teaching to study mineralogy and widen his knowledge of chemistry. He has taught agriculture and apiculture to the villagers of Momchilovo. He leads a very simple and modest bachelor life. He has a considerable collection of Natural History specimens. He is an ardent mountaineer, a lover of nature and a very keen shot.

The Colonel sighed; then he pressed the button of the bell beside him and told his aide to ask his two agents to come in.

The Colonel looked up at the two Captains and motioned them to be seated.

'I have read your reports,' he said. 'In fact, several times. Before I discuss them with you, as I wish to do, here are some facts that you ought to know.

'Our technical department tells me that the fingerprints on the pieces of broken glass you sent in, Captain Kovachev, are undoubtedly those of Metodi Parashkevov. Similarly there are prints on the cigarette stub which in all probability are those of Parashkevov's right thumb, though they are not clear enough for this to be absolutely certain. The stub has been crushed by an iron-shod heel—and Parashkevov wears shoes with iron-shod heels.

'Add this to the rest of the circumstantial evidence and it

would appear that the case is pretty simple—and proved. Yet Captain Zakhov not only seems to doubt the evidence, but believes that Parashkevov is innocent. Why?'

'May I smoke, sir?' Zakhov said, and when the Colonel nodded assent he lit a cigarette and took two or three pulls at it in silence.

'This business is a good bit more complicated than it appears. It is tempting to accept the circumstantial evidence and let the man go to his death. But that will neither recover the map nor find the transmitter and those who work it—which, I take it, is why we were sent to Momchilovo. Evidence apart, we have both seen Metodi Parashkevov and, apparently, formed contradictory opinions of him. What makes you, Kovachev, think him a criminal type?'

'I don't,' Kovachev said. 'He's a criminal, at least I think he is, because he is a spy, but I think he is an idealist. These days people turn traitor for only two reasons: to get money or to serve a cause. The latter are idealists, often highly educated, and I believe that Parashkevov comes within this category. He may be educated, but he's a pretty clumsy spy.'

Colonel Manov's doctors had told him to give up smoking and when his hand now went involuntarily to the pocket of his tunic, only to find it empty, Zakhov noticed the gesture and held out his own packet. Gratefully the Colonel took one and accepted a light.

'I see,' said Zakhov. 'Then our opinions of him are not so different. It's rather on the interpretation of the facts that we do not see eye to eye. Wouldn't it be a good idea if Captain Kovachev gave his interpretation and I tried to explain where, and why, I disagree?'

'Over to you, Kovachev,' Colonel Manov said.

'The time was between one and two in the morning—we can't know exactly because the sentry did not have a watch. Metodi Parashkevov returned from the Zmeitza, rough and difficult country for those not used to it and arduous at night even for those who are. His route took him, as usual, through the courtyard of the house in which the Geological Survey has its offices; there he exchanged a few words with the sentry, but not many, for he was in a hurry. He took a few paces into the darkness, circled back and hit the sentry on the back of the head with some iron object, knocking him out. He then took a towel and a bottle of chloroform from his pocket, drenched the towel with chloroform and wrapped it tightly round the man's head, thus assuring himself of several hours' liberty of action.

'He then went to one of the windows of the quarters occupied by the Geological Survey, which, with his height, it was simple for him to reach. He tapped a pane of glass with, probably, the same iron object, making a hole large enough for him to put his hand through and grip the iron bar behind; then, bracing his feet against the wall, he removed the pieces of glass. That done, he dropped to the ground again to rest his muscles, and lit a cigarette which he would naturally hide in the hollow of his hand. He then stamped the cigarette out with his heel, hoisted himself up to the window again and started filing through the bar with a steel file. The bar being made of softish iron, it did not take him more than ten minutes or so to file through it. He twisted it until he had an opening large enough to climb through. I suppose that the whole business took him only fifteen to twenty minutes. Inside the offices, he used a skeleton key to open the cupboard where the secret documents and money are kept, found the map he wanted and, seeing the money, took that in order to try and make it look a case of theft rather than espionage. Then he went home as if nothing had happened and got into bed, but without undressing. After a few hours' sleep, he got up at dawn and began packing his rucksack, ostensibly for a climbing or shooting expedition, but in reality in order to hide his bottle of chloroform and perhaps hoping to give himself an alibi by not being in the village when the crime was discovered. Unfortunately for him, he was arrested before he could even finish packing his rucksack.

'What weak points can you find in that?'

Captain Kovachev sat back in his chair, a satisfied smile on his face, and lit a cigarette.

Zakhov looked at the Colonel, who nodded: then he got to his feet and began walking up and down the room in slow, small steps, to and fro between the window and the door.

'First,' he said, 'the distance between the ground and the bottom of the glass in the window is exactly eight feet, so that though a tall man might be able to break the glass with a short metal object, he could not get his hand through and grasp an iron bar behind it. Parashkevov is a man of no more than medium height and to break that glass he would have had to use a stick or rod of some kind, or thrown a stone—all rather noisy ways of achieving his end.

'We know that the frame of the window was an external one; the actual glass protruding a finger's breadth beyond the wall. Now however you break a window like that, if it is done from the outside, bits of glass, large or small, must fall onto the ground beneath it. Some may be small enough to escape immediate notice, but there will inevitably be larger pieces that will be clearly visible. The fact is that no pieces of glass have been found under the window, neither fragments nor even powdery particles. I have been over the ground with a magnifying glass and there is no trace.

'You contend that the culprit inserted an arm, hoisted himself up and remained there by bracing his leg against the wall, while he removed the jagged bits of glass from the frame. Now, if you brace a foot against a wall, especially one shod with iron at toe and heel as are the boots we are told Parashkevov was wearing, you cannot do so without leaving scratches or other marks. I have examined the wall both under the window and to either side and have been unable, even with the magnifying glass, to find any such marks; in fact, no fresh marks of any kind. Even if the culprit had removed his boots or shoes, the friction must have left abrasions or some marks, particles of wool if he had done so in stockinged feet, or of skin if he had been barefoot. There is *nothing*. I have examined the roughcast surface, even photographed it and enlarged the picture; here are the prints, numbered in sequence. You will see that there are no marks of any kind that could be attributed to a foot, shod, stockinged or bare. The prints cover the whole surface of the wall under the window from three feet above the ground.'

Zakhov passed the photographs to his Colonel and lit a cigarette. There was a faint smile round his lips.

'Next you say that while he held himself hoisted up with the hand that grasped the iron bar, he removed the broken glass with his other hand and threw the pieces onto the floor of the room. Wouldn't it have been much easier and more sensible to throw them onto the ground, outside? But never mind, that's a mere detail.

'Let's suppose the man breaking in did remove the pieces of glass and throw them onto the floor. What did one find there? Two large pieces about a foot across and a dozen or so smaller pieces mostly a hand's breadth in size. Now, you must remember firstly that the floors of the rooms in Iliazov's house are tiled, and secondly that the distance from the windowsill to these tiles is five feet. If you drop or throw a piece of glass from a height of five feet onto stone, the glass will break into pieces much smaller than any of those you found and sent in.

'Then you say that the villain filed through the bar across the window with a steel file and then twisted the bar sufficiently to make an opening through which he could climb. The bar has been filed through and twisted, it is true, but the

39

file mark is broader on the inside of the bar, that towards the interior of the room, than on the outside, showing that the bar was filed from the inside. If you were clinging to the outside by one hand, it would be very difficult, if not impossible, to file through an iron bar from the inside. Again, having filed through the bar and wanting to bend it so as to allow you to climb through, what would you do? You would push it away from you. In fact, if you were clinging to a wall with one hand, you would not be able to pull anything very far towards you at all. And how would he have got inside with the bent bar pointing outward? No! You said you thought him clumsy and stupid for not having hidden his chloroform in time, but if he had behaved in this way he—or anyone else— would have been worse than stupid. Such actions would have been those of a half-wit.

'Another thing: could anyone have squeezed through such a window without leaving on the rough surfaces of the window-frame or the filed ends of the bar fibres from his clothing or particles of his own skin? Here again my faithful magnifying glass has been brought into play and revealed nothing: no fibres of cloth, no tiny bits of skin, no blood. But—and this is my last point—if the man had held the bar in his hand, as indeed he must have, it too should bear his fingerprints. There are none to be found. If he had thought to wipe them off, why did he not also wipe the glass he had touched? If he was wearing gloves to obviate the need to wipe off fingerprints, why are there prints on those two—and only two—pieces of glass? In actual fact that bar is a very rusty one and the rust in the middle shows slight traces of rubbing, as if subjected to some sort of pressure, and on the windowsill, among the iron filings, I found these filaments of blue wool.' Zakhov produced a piece of paper from his pocket, unfolded it and placed it on the desk in front of the Colonel. 'It seems to me beyond doubt that whoever filed through that bar wore gloves to do so. He at least was neither clumsy nor all that stupid. Blue woollen gloves. But I don't think they were worn by Metodi Parashkevov.'

Zakhov flung himself into a chair and lit a cigarette.

'And the other conclusion, of course,' he went on, 'is that the window was broken and the bar filed through from inside the room and no one crawled through it at all. All that was just a red herring.'

'All right, suppose it was just a red herring, as you call it,' Kovachev said. 'Parashkevov is still the only one who could have knocked out and chloroformed the sentry. He may well have got himself a skeleton key or a copy of the door key.'

'But if he had, why break the window, make sure there were *his* fingerprints on some of the glass, file through the bar and put on gloves to do so? It doesn't make sense.'

'No, Kovachev,' Colonel Manov said. 'There's more to this than meets the eye. I'm not saying that Parashkevov is not the perpetrator, but as far as the mode of entry goes, Zakhov would seem to be right. Anyway, Zakhov, how do you see the case at this juncture?'

Zakhov got to his feet and resumed his slow pacing between the window and the door.

'Someone whose identity has not yet been established, so let's call him X, was given the mission of purloining this important plan, sketch or whatever it was, from the Geological Survey. Or, another possibility, he may have had no mission, but merely wanted to compromise someone so severely as, perhaps, even to cause his death. This someone may have represented a danger to him or been an obstacle to his achieving some important aim or objective, and so he wished to remove him. Or, one could envisage a combination of the two.

'In some way that I cannot yet explain, this X managed to get hold of two pieces of glass bearing the fingerprints of Metodi Parashkevov—whom he wished to have out of his way.

Then, during the night of 22-3 August, he went to the Geological Survey, having knocked out the sentry, and opened the door with a key—he must have had a key because he locked it behind him again when he left. Once inside, he opened the window, broke the glass, pocketed some of it and substituted the two pieces he had brought with him which he knew to bear the fingerprints of his victim; then he filed through the bar. And twisted it out, as he thought he had to do, if people were to think that entry had been effected that way. He then broke open the cupboard, got his map, saw the money and took it to make it look like theft, and left, locking the door behind him.

'Don't shift about on your chair, Kovachev! I know you're dying to say, "And what about the cigarette stub, the chloroform and towel?"

'Imagine for a moment that we three are inhabitants of Momchilovo and that Manov possesses some potassium cyanide, a few secret agent's capsules from the war, and that this is known to certain people. I too know it and, wanting to kill my colleague, Kovachev, I get hold of a pill or two and use them on him. Nobody knows that I have such a thing and so, at any rate at first, no one suspects me; but they do suspect Manov because they remember that he had the cyanide in his possession. Thus X—who knew that Metodi Parashkevov had chloroform and was the only one in Momchilovo to do so, which means that he has excellent knowledge of local conditions—sees it as an excellent weapon to use against him, and does so. In fact, X has killed two birds with one stone: he has accomplished his mission and thrown suspicion, if nothing more, on someone else. But, of course, the chloroform X used was some that he had in his possession. As for the towel, I imagine that X purloined that during the night of 22-3 August. The cigarette stub is a pure chance—and a lucky one for X. Obviously it belonged to the schoolmaster, who probably threw it down as he passed and stamped it out with his heel.

'X, as I see him, is quite clever and imaginative; certainly not clumsy or inept. For all his intelligence, though, he has made some unpardonable mistakes. But if criminals did not make mistakes, their crimes would never be discovered, would they? Our concern is to see that X's mistakes should be discovered in time.

'X's plan for throwing dust in our eyes was quite an ingenious one, but his implementation of it was not good: he failed to make any scratches or marks on the outside wall such as would have been made by a foot; he forgot to throw some bits of glass onto the ground at the foot of the outside wall beneath the window; it was silly of him to file the bar from the inside and push it out, instead of pulling it in. Similarly, it was not very intelligent to have *large* pieces of glass on the stone floor. If he had not made these mistakes, I believe that I, like Kovachev, would have thought Parashkevov guilty, but, as it is, I am sure that he is not.'

Zakhov halted his pacing and looked out of the window. His eye was caught by the figure of a girl so like Sia that, involuntarily, he leaned forward, as if that would help him to get a better view. The girl was not Sia, though very like her, only a good bit younger. The thought crossed Zakhov's mind that he would not mind spending his leave with that girl. Then he checked himself. Don't develop a taste for young girls. At forty you're too old for that! he told himself and, turning, went back to his chair. The Colonel, he noticed, was rummaging in his drawer in the hope of finding a forgotten cigarette and Kovachev was gnawing at his lip. Now his amour propre is writhing like a crushed snake, Zakhov told himself, and felt a wry sort of pity—as well as a momentary stab of Schadenfreude.

Meanwhile the Colonel had found a cigarette and lit it airily; then he looked up at his two captains.

'It seems to me that you, Zakhov, are on the right track,' he said. 'You, Kovachev, have rather tended to jump to conclusions—as the man intended you to do,' he said. 'Anyway,

I don't see that this affair needs more than one of you dealing with it, so you'd better carry on on your own, Zakhov. As you're owed some leave, Kovachev, you could take it now, if that would suit you.'

Captain Kovachev got to his feet, rather red in the face. The Colonel stood up behind his desk and held out his hand.

'Have a good leave,' he said.

When the door closed behind Captain Kovachev, Colonel Manov turned to Zakhov and said, 'I told my wife that I should be home for lunch, so as we've still got a lot to discuss you'd better come along too. I'll just give her a ring and warn her and ask her to put a couple of bottles in the fridge.'

This was the sort of invitation one cannot refuse and Zakhov did not even attempt to do so. He had already said goodbye to his leave and, probably, to Sia. He could not tell her the truth; and just to say, as he must, that a new archaeological find had been made which he must investigate and that it was in a part of the country, which he could not specify, to which she could not accompany him—well, could you imagine a lamer excuse than that? She would draw the only possible conclusion, even though the wrong one, take umbrage and that would be that.

Colonel Manov finished telephoning and turned to Zakhov again.

'What we still don't *know* is that the theft of the plan and the coded messages are the work of the same person or of the same group or organization. It is highly probable, but we have yet to establish the fact and neither problem can be satisfactorily solved until we have done so.

'As head of counter-espionage I must take the view that this—and finding out what happened to the plan—is more important than proving the innocence of Metodi Parashkevov, which, I think, you have proved. He, poor fellow, is in a thoroughly unenviable situation—a step or two from the gallows.

You know what these rural magistrates are like: circumstantial evidence and a few fingerprints and the thing's proven. There's no arguing with them when they have such "evidence" thrust under their noses. Those are "facts" and it won't matter to them whether a bar has been pushed out or pulled in, once filed through it can go either way and which way it goes proves nothing. So your poor schoolteacher is in a nasty fix until you can find the actual culprit. Let's hope that Justice will live up to its reputation for slowness in his case.

'But, of course, there's more to it than just his escaping the gallows or not. If he doesn't, your culprit, X, will have achieved all his aims: he will remain at liberty with a completely free hand—and all we shall know is that there is a clever and very efficient spy on that part of the frontier—with all that that means.

'Now let's go and have lunch and lay our plans.'

The two men emerged from the door of the unobtrusive building in which the counter-espionage organization had its offices, and into the sunshine. Looking thoroughly ordinary and unmilitary in their civilian suits, they crossed to the other side of the street and stood facing the great Alexander Nevsky Memorial Church, looking quite small away at the end of the long street, as they waited for the tram that would take them out to the suburban villa in which the Colonel lived.

8

AFTER A LENGTHY LUNCH with the Colonel, Avakum Zakhov went to the library of the Institute of Archaeology and looked up Momchilovo and its surroundings. Strangely, there was more than he had expected and he made quite a number of notes.

Back at home, he had to face the question of Sia, whom he was due to meet the following day, before leaving for their joint holiday in three days' time. Sia was no fool, and he had felt that his story was not good enough to be told verbally, so that he could neither meet her nor telephone her. An ordinary letter would not reach her in time, so that he must either send a telegram or an express letter. He could not have her waiting for him at their rendezvous in vain. In Zakhov's scale of values, courtesy came before most things. Courtesy was culture, and if he considered himself anything it was a man of culture. A telegram, he told himself, would be too curt, official, bureaucratic. He must write and send it express. So after chewing a pen for some minutes, he wrote:

SIA [Without an accompanying adjective that could mean a lot or little depending on how you read it]—I have suddenly been given the chance of going on an important dig. This could mean a lot to me in the future and I dare not say no, though it means that I must postpone my leave. I am sure you will understand and approve. I expect to be back in about a month and shall look forward to seeing you then. Do have a good holiday.

He read it through a couple of times, improved the shape of a letter or two and, feeling satisfied that it said neither too much nor too little, wrote 'Yours ever, AVAKUM,' underneath in a bold hand. He then laid the letter on the table to be dispatched first thing in the morning.

It was late when he had finished and he crawled into bed and fell into a deep sleep, from which the alarm roused him, greatly reluctant, at half-past six. Stumbling through to the kitchen, he put his head under the cold tap, shaved and went back to his room, where he dressed carefully in a grey lightweight suit and blue tie, which he tied with his usual exaggerated care. Dress was one of his foibles. He could not bear not having a ticket pocket inside his jacket pocket. He abhorred dusty or dirty shoes, while a badly tied tie made him nervous and irritable.

Then he got out an enormous hold-all, which he proceeded to fill with a suit, another pair of shoes, shirts and underwear, a variety of little bottles labelled with chemical formulae, two boxes of cartridges, a short-handled file in a leather case, his shaving things, and so on. Then he closed it, locked it and tied on a small label on which he had written a few letters mixed with figures. Then he picked up the telephone and had a short conversation with Colonel Manov, telling him that he would first check on Parashkevov's story and origins and would the colonel in the meantime let him have particulars of all civilian members of the survey, their wives, families and other connections.

A quarter of an hour later, a duty sergeant from the Department reported at Zakhov's house and was told to take the hold-all and have it and a portable two-way radio sent to the police station at Smolyan to wait for Zakhov to claim them.

Next, hearing noises coming from the kitchen, Zakhov went to see his landlady. She was accustomed to his absences and scarcely needed to be told that he was going on an archaeological expedition. He paid her two months' rent in advance and told her that he would send her more if his absence was prolonged, but that he scarcely thought that would be necessary. She told him to be careful of snakes and asked if he had remembered to pack some quinine.

It was eight o'clock when he left home and an hour later he was in the plane for Varna. Varna—on the Black Sea. How lovely if that had really been his destination. Above the heavy cloudbanks, they crossed the Central Mountains in the dip between the peaks of Baba and Vezhan. The plane droned on above a polar landscape. The 'snow' looked so solid, you could have sworn you could have travelled it with a sledge and dog-team. Nothing moved down there but the black shadow of the plane.

They landed at Gorna Oryakhovitsa, just beyond the last of the foothills, and Zakhov alighted. He had no luggage; just a raincoat thrown over his shoulder. He took several deep breaths: this was proper air! How different to the diesel fumes of the city! This was home—or very nearly. Tarnovo, where Avakum Zakhov had been born, was only an hour's drive away. He told himself that he might be able to pay it a visit on his way back. Then he walked across to a telephone booth and went inside it.

Zakhov waited until the plane had taken off again on its way to Varna before he emerged from the telephone box, hands up to his face in the act of lighting a cigarette, blue eyes taking in everything and everyone in the now almost empty hall. Then he walked out of the building and set off down the road leading to the town. In the main square his eye was caught by a big grey Pobeda, its tall young driver leaning against the bonnet, jaws moving and one hand clutching a handful of sunflower seeds.

Zakhov stopped in front of him.

'Can I have some of those?' he said.

The young man went on chewing, his face expressionless.

'I want to go to Targovichté,' Zakhov said.

At that the young man stopped chewing, clicked his heels together and saluted smartly.

'My orders are to be entirely at your disposal,' he said, opening the door.

'Good. Then off we go!' Zakhov settled himself in the corner of the back seat and the Pobeda sped off smoothly. Soon they were out of the town and in open country. The road ran through vineyards and field after field of vegetables, but Zakhov, preoccupied with his own thoughts, failed to see them. If the fields had been full of *kazanluk* roses he would scarcely have noticed the wonderful smell. The village of Arbanassi appeared ahead and a minute or two later they were in among its old houses. This was such familiar ground that Zakhov closed his eyes: he knew where he was without looking: 9 September Square, now the Town Hall, right, now left, now he was passing the house he once lived in. He wondered if the vine and the three lilacs still grew in the little courtyard. Then they were through the village and out in open country again, heading for Kozarvevetz. For a time the road followed the river, running between interminable vineyards. The road looked black in the sunlight.

Targovichté. They pulled up at the police station, and while Zakhov was inside telephoning the driver again took up his lounging position against the bonnet and his jaws resumed their slow grinding motion. The heat was intense and the air between the houses heavy and suffocatingly full of the smell of hot macadam and dust. Leaving the town, they turned off the main highway and continued due east down a minor road. Here the car bumped and swayed, for the driver seemed to see no reason to reduce speed just because of a few potholes, and his poor passenger had to put out both hands and let his arms act as lateral shock-absorbers. Thus it was almost three o'clock before they reached the outskirts of Preslav. Which would attract least attention, Zakhov wondered: to drive into the sleepy old place in a strange car or to appear on foot, an obvious stranger? He decided that the latter course was preferable, so he stopped the car and got out, telling the driver that he had no further need of him. He stood there watching as the big car turned and drove off in a cloud of dust back the way it had come, before the dust of its first passage had had time to settle. Then he turned and strode off into the town.

The road was lined with fruit trees. There was not a breath of air, nothing to stir the leaves on the trees, let alone blow the dust off them. He passed a big vineyard and wondered if that was the one that had belonged to Metodi Parashkevov's family. He had come to check up on the man and find out about him and his antecedents. He hoped he would find nothing to upset his theories.

Avakum booked himself in at the big hotel in the new square. Then he waited until the hands of his watch pointed to ten to three and, going outside, told the aged driver of an equally aged cab, with peeling paint, to drive him to the old town.

The cab had soon rattled and jolted out of the concrete functionalism of the new town and was rolling through the park that separates it from the old town, one or two of the houses in which still date back to medieval times, when Preslav was a Slav settlement. At one time, indeed, it had been the capital of Bulgaria. As soon as he caught sight of the monument to Boris Sirov, a local hero, Zakhov halted the cab, told the driver to drive on and wait for him in the shade of the trees of the avenue beyond the open space in which the statue stood. He then strolled towards the latter, as if he had nothing else in mind but enjoyment of those pleasant surroundings. As he reached the monument a man appeared from the side, a thick-set man wearing a white waistcoat and black trousers under a black jacket. Hardly the dress for this weather, Zakhov thought, and noted that the man's forehead and upper lip were beaded with sweat. The man smiled and Zakhov realized that they knew each other, had worked together briefly some years before.

The two men stood facing each other. Zakhov looked round: apart from the cab-driver there wasn't a soul in sight.

'I want all the information you can get me about Metodi Parashkevov, who was born here in 1921. His parents owned a big vineyard on the outskirts of the town. The father died in 1945, the mother in 1946. He was the only child. I'll make the routine search in the registers and archives, but I want all the information you can get me about the family, its associates, connections, reputation, general background. Let me have what you can get by midnight tonight. If I need to see you again, I shall breakfast in the café opposite the hotel round about eight; if not, I shall breakfast in the hotel.'

Zakhov strolled on towards the avenue, got into the cab and had himself driven to the Museum. For the next hour he became the archaeologist. He then walked back from the old town to the registrar's and the police and made his routine check on Metodi Parashkevov. This merely confirmed the facts he had already been given, and to his relief, provided no information that invalidated his theory of what had happened at Momchilovo.

Back at the hotel, Zakhov found the first interim report from his stocky little helper. A further envelope was delivered about eleven o'clock that night, just before the hotel shut its door. Tired from the day's travel, Zakhov went to his bed shortly afterwards and slept well.

He had asked to be roused at half-past seven and by a quarter past eight he was ensconced in a corner of the veranda of the café opposite the hotel, having breakfast. There his little man joined him and delivered a further report, which Zakhov stuffed into his pocket. He then went for a stroll round the walls of the old town, the remains of the fortifications put up in the Middle Ages when they had withstood more than one Byzantine attack and, later, even proved an obstacle to the Turks. Although this would have been a place to interest Zakhov the archaeologist, it was the counter-espionage officer who strolled along the grassy ramparts there, his gaze turned inward, where it was concentrated on the twenty-five letters and figures which comprised the last message from the clandestine transmitter in the Zmeitza, and which the experts in Sofia had still not managed to decipher.

Returning to the hotel, Zakhov found an envelope from Sofia brought by special messenger from Kolarovgrad. He went up to his room only to find that the chambermaid was just starting to do it, so he went downstairs and out into the square, where he walked across to the cab rank, got into the same shabby old cab as he had hired the previous day and told the man to drive him to the ruins of the old monastery across on the right bank of the Ticha. There he found a secluded sunny spot among some trees and sat down on the grass to see what news Sofia had for him.

First, the negative information that the monitoring service had reported no further transmission from the Karabair area and that the code was still unbroken.

The Survey had two civilian members: Boyan Icherenski, aged forty-two, married; wife, Victoria, living in Plovdiv, where husband goes each weekend. Icherenski born at Burgas on Black Sea. Father, died in 1943, well-to-do importer of olive oil and Mediterranean fruits. No surviving relatives.

The second civilian member of the Survey was Kuzman Naumov Christoforov, aged thirty-eight. Mining engineer. Unmarried. Details to follow. This was little.

Zakhov settled himself more comfortably in a patch of shade and lit a pipe. He liked to pretend that a pipe helped him to think. First, he must test his own theory to see if he could find any flaws in it. As he reviewed it, he puffed at his pipe, slowly at first, then faster and faster, causing a couple of magpies to fly off chattering their disgust. High up above his head an eagle was circling, small but unmistakable in that clear air.

The air beneath the trees was heavy with the smell of baked earth, dead leaves and resinous bushes. Near by was a heap of stones that would have made an excellent home for a snake or two. This was the monastery where in the tenth century Tsar

Simeon, who was called, or liked to hear himself called, the 'good monk', lived for a while after the bloody battle of Ankhialo, dreaming perhaps of seeing himself on the throne of Byzantium which he was claiming. He had made Preslav his capital, where he lived in considerable splendour, not quite consistent with his religious aspirations.

What worried Zakhov was why the mysterious X had gone to such lengths to put suspicion on Metodi Parashkevov. Was it a question of personal vengeance? His researches into Parashkevov's past had yielded nothing to suggest this view. Could it be a local feud? Something of recent origin, the start of which could only be discovered at Momchilovo?

But suppose his theory of how and why the window had been broken, the bar filed through and the theft carried out was not correct? Suppose that the reverse was the case, on the mathematical principle of testing conclusions by assuming the opposite to be true. The absence of pieces of glass or rough-cast on the ground, the bar being filed from the inside and then bent outwards, the big pieces of glass on the tiles—on the face of it, these were 'mistakes' such as the criminal traditionally makes, yet there is nothing to say that they were not made on purpose to make those investigating the theft of the map think that they were intended as a red herring; if that were so, then Parashkevov could be representing himself as the victim of an unknown trying to attach blame to someone else, whereas in actual fact Parashkevov and X were the same person. You could not absolutely rule that out, Zakhov supposed, but it was an appalling risk for anyone to run; the likelihood of the bluffer ending on the gallows seemed so great that Zakhov could not see how any but a very desperate person would agree to take it.

So far there was nothing to show that Parashkevov was other than he had first thought him; it remained to be seen what he would find at Kolarovgrad, where Parashkevov had been teaching. Returning to the hotel, Zakhov rang up the stocky little man with the white waistcoat and told him to send any further information he might obtain to Kolarovgrad. Then he summoned a car and set off for there himself.

Although he had often seen photographs of the ancient town with its houses arranged in tiers like the seats in an amphitheatre, its great walls and thirteen gates, he had never been there before, and the artistic side to his nature shrank from the sight of the new canneries and factories through which he had to drive before he even caught sight of the minarets of the Tumbul mosque. He was so dispirited by the ugliness of this modern growth that he went on to Madara, age-old and comparatively unspoilt, and put up at the inn there. From a public callbox he rang up the police at Kolarovgrad who, forewarned, readily agreed to put a man onto searching out the associates and connections of Parashkevov during his years in the town.

He found that the ruins of the old fortress of Madara acted as balm to his soul and, having smoked a pipe there, he returned to the inn and summoned a car to take him to his rendezvous with the local detective.

Zakhov would have been horrified if you had suggested that he was a gourmet, but he liked spacious surroundings and good food and, when the mood was upon him, often indulged these tastes. On this occasion he had told the man to meet him at the big and expensive restaurant in Kyoshkov Park. In this delightful setting Zakhov wined and dined discreetly, while he waited for his informant with fresh news, perhaps, about Metodi Parashkevov.

The reports he received that night and the following morning revealed nothing beyond the fact that Parashkevov was a quiet, intelligent, well-behaved person, who took his job very seriously and did his best. That he was patriotic and loyal there seemed no doubt, nor that he was highly intelligent and had a considerable knowledge of various sciences: geology, chemistry, mineralogy, far beyond that of the amateur.

The next place on Zakhov's list was Provadia, where Parashkevov had also been employed. There he set going his routine search into the man's past and gave instructions for the results to be communicated to him at Plovdiv. A car took him to Varna, where he was just in time to catch the evening plane for Plovdiv. (He never even saw the sea until he was up circling the airport.)

The car that awaited him at Plovdiv airport took him to a private house in the residential part of the town, where he was given a big, sunny room with a veranda and its own bathroom. He was waited on by a taciturn old crone, who never came out of her kitchen until called. In his big, bright room he found a huge pile of papers awaiting him: details of all the frontier incidents that had taken place over the last few years, texts of signals, reports of strange or suspect happenings on the southern frontier. It took him most of the night to go through all this, and the sun was already up before he finally got in between the sheets.

It was late when he woke and he had only just finished breakfast when a car arrived with two policemen in civilian clothes to remove the files he had been studying. They brought a sealed envelope from Sofia. Colonel Manov had no news of great interest, but he gave further details of Boyan Icherenski's wife, Victoria, née Stratev.

The Stratevs were an old Plovdiv family, the chief member of which in the twentieth century had been one Ivan Stefanov Stratev, who had an agency selling imported agricultural machinery. He had married a Plovdiv girl, Illaria Pechenikova, who was a good bit his junior. They had a son, Illary. When Illary was aged four, that is in 1922, Illaria ran away to join a foreign diplomat, a member of his country's consular service, who had been transferred from Plovdiv to a post in another country. Ivan Stefanov divorced his wife and six years later married again. This second wife, Maria, née Benkovski, was the daughter of a high government official. She presented Ivan with a daughter, Victoria. Victoria's mother died shortly before the outbreak of the Second World War and her father towards the end of 1944. There were unconfirmed rumours that Illaria, still abroad, had been abandoned by her consular lover and had later married a Bulgarian resident in the same city.

Zakhov the archaeologist had been in Plovdiv several times, but he was more interested in it as the Eumolpiada of the ancient Thracians or even as the Trimontium of the Romans than as the industrial centre it has now become, so there was no temptation for him to linger there. A visit to the police and the local army H.Q. occupied most of the rest of the day, and after a scratch meal he set off for Smolyan in a service car. Luckily the road from his lodgings avoided what he called the 'inevitable hideosities' of industrial life and before long he saw the lights of Assenovgrad ahead of him and knew that soon he would be in the heart of the Rhodopes, the Mountains of Orpheus. In the dark, the trees and bushes crowding in upon the sides of the road and the steep sides of the cuttings revealed little to the probing headlights but the ribbon of the road ahead and the occasional sparkling streak of falling water. Had he been travelling in his other capacity, Zakhov would have quoted Ovid to himself and tried to imagine the scene in those distant days; as it was, a sudden jolt prompted the thought that though the road in those days would not have been so wide, the surface was probably no worse. Then his mind went back to the matter in hand, and, as he was carried through the dark mountains, he went over the details yielded by his researches of the last two days. The resultant portrait of Metodi Parashkevov was that of a man whose parents had never taken part in politics, but who had been liberal rather than conservative, and certainly not reactionary. His relatives—none very close were still alive—were all members of farming co-operatives, and two of his cousins had been awarded silver medals for developing a successful new dessert grape. Metodi Parashkevov seemed to have followed his parents' example and held aloof from politics, though there were several instances of his having sympathized with pupils who had 'progressive' ideas. On the other hand, there was no evidence at all of any sympathy for the people or ideas of the Right.

Most reports described the schoolmaster as a gentle and extremely modest man, whose way of life was, if anything, austere and who tended to disregard his own comfort and convenience. He was described as taciturn and uncommunicative and of rather a difficult temperament, yet without being arrogant or uncouth. One and all regarded him as a born schoolmaster. His hobbies appeared to be chemistry, geology, of which he had a considerable knowledge, and, above all, shooting. Wherever he had taught, he had made for the pupils of the school an excellent collection of the local stones, crystals and other items of geological interest. One or two people had hazarded the assertion that he had remained a bachelor just because he spent so much time on collecting geological specimens and so much money on books, scientific instruments and chemicals.

Hunting and shooting appeared to be inherited pastimes. His father had been a keen sportsman and his grandfather had been renowned far and wide as a great killer of wolves. The schoolmaster had also studied taxidermy and presented all the schools at which he had taught with stuffed specimens of the local animals and birds all mounted on the correct background, which was most attractively and accurately depicted.

It was not easy to see who or what had decided him to give up teaching and go to Sofia. There was relatively little information—even from Colonel Manov—about the man's two years there in the capital. Apparently he had lived there on the proceeds of the sale of the family vineyard. He had bought a sporting gun from a visiting foreigner, probably an Englishman as the gun was the work of a London gunsmith called Holland (in the report the name was typed twice, which must have been a mistake). He had during this period applied for a post at the Institute of Mines and Geology, but he had been turned down, the record of his interview being marked: 'Is not sufficiently active politically.' He had had a room during this period in the flat of an engine-driver, who had said of him, 'Had bloody little to say for himself, unsociable sort of bloke, kept himself to himself, always had his nose in a bloody book, or was off somewhere with his gun. But he was generous with what he shot, always giving it away. He loaded his own cartridges. The only thing my wife disliked about him was the way he filled his room with pebbles and stones. And his table was covered with bottles and jars. One day he bought himself a microscope and that evening we actually heard him humming to himself, he was so pleased with it.

'He never had visitors. Paid his rent on the dot. He was a bit miserly about his clothes. He seemed to grudge spending money on them; and my wife, who washed and mended for him, was always turning collars and cuffs.

'But we got on all right together and my wife was very sorry when he told us that he was going to the country to be a teacher.'

It really did look as though Metodi Parashkevov and the sentry's assailant, X, were not the same person. Also, it was most unlikely that Parashkevov was anything but a loyal patriot, let alone an enemy agent. Why had he gone back to teaching? Merely because his money was coming to an end and he had failed to get the job at the Institute of Mines? Why not?

The car tore on through the night. Avakum Zakhov wedged himself into a corner of the back seat and fell into a restless doze.

9

There was no light in any of the windows when they reached Smolyan, and it was some time before the night porter would respond to their knocking at the door of the hotel. As Zakhov drew the curtain across the window of the room, there was enough light in the sky for him to discern the dark outline of the wooded mountainside that formed the sloping wall of the bowl in which the little town lay, and he could hear the song of the river, small and unassuming there, but big and important by the time it reached the great lake.

Morning brought breakfast on the terrace and, via the police station, an envelope from Sofia. Colonel Manov, it appeared, had nothing more to add about his researches into Metodi Parashkevov, so he sent Zakhov extracts from the transcript of his interrogations by the examining magistrate, which he thought threw some light on the man's character and attitude of mind. Also included was the basic dossier of Kuzman Christoforov. As soon as he had read this, Zakhov dismissed it from his mind. Christoforov, he felt, was quite uninteresting and capable of only the most subordinate role.

The monitoring service had reported what it had taken to be an attempt to call up the clandestine transmitter at Momchilovo, but this had not answered. The call had been put out thirty minutes earlier than previous transmissions, which perhaps accounted for the Zmeitza's failure to respond.

At his first examination of Metodi Parashkevov, the examining magistrate followed the usual procedure of inviting the accused to tell him about himself. According to the transcript Parashkevov had sighed and said:

'What is there for me to say that you haven't already found out? I have nothing to say that can interest you.'

'That is for us to judge.'

But the accused had remained silent and refused to say anything more.

Then he was asked, 'How do you explain your frequent excursions into the mountains?'

'I went out shooting.'

'If you are shooting, surely you carry a gun? You went out quite often without one, didn't you?'

'Of course I did. My interests are not confined to shooting.'

'What other interests have you, then?'

'Nature study for one,' the accused replied.

Later, the magistrate said to him, 'You say that on the evening of 22 August you went for a walk to the west of the village. Yet there are witnesses who say that they met you on the road that leads to the village of Lakité, that is in the opposite direction to what you told us. Why did you try to mislead us?'

No answer.

During the second interrogation, the examining magistrate at one point said to the accused, 'Last year in a skirmish with the police a deviationist agent, Kademov from the village of Lakité, was shot and killed. Did you know him?'

'I did,' the accused replied. 'He had a good eye and a steady hand. He was a good hunter.'

'Did you often hunt together?'

'Together—never. But we met up on the mountains on several occasions.'

'Can you remember when was the last occasion?' Very calmly the accused replied, 'I think it must have been a year before he was killed.'

'And did you meet him elsewhere after the last encounter? In the mountains?'

'I would perhaps have done so on the day of his funeral, only I felt too lazy to walk all the way to Lakité,' the accused said, smiling.

In the course of the third interrogation of Metodi Parashkevov, the examining magistrate said, 'Comrade Parashkevov, you deny having taken part in the assault on the sentry and the breaking into the offices of the Geological Survey at Momchilovo, but if you did not, how do you explain the presence of your fingerprints on the pieces of broken glass found there?'

'If I were a detective, I have no doubt I should be able to find an answer to your question,' the accused said with a shrug. Then after a moment's thought, he added, 'I suppose it would have been possible for someone to have taken my fingers while I was asleep, then gone to Iliazov's House, broken the window, put my prints on the glass and come back and put my fingers back in place again. Don't you think it might?'

'That is just being ridiculous!' the magistrate said.

'No more ridiculous than your accusation of me!' the accused retorted, giving him an indignant look.

The magistrate then produced the bottle of chloroform, the towel and the cigarette stub, and said, 'Do you recognize these objects?'

'Well, of course I do!' the accused exclaimed. 'At least, the chloroform bottle and the towel are mine. I bought them with my own money. As for the cigarette end,' he added after a moment's thought, 'I couldn't swear to its being mine. They all look exactly alike.'

'Don't worry about the cigarette end,' the magistrate said. 'We have had it examined and the experts have discovered the mark of your shoe on it.'

'Then it must be mine too,' the accused said, and smiled again. 'Actually, I remember that I did throw a cigarette down when I was passing the house, probably not far from the window, and as there was a stiff wind blowing I trod it out to prevent any risk of fire.'

'You have a good memory,' the magistrate observed, 'so, no doubt, you will have no difficulty in recalling how your towel came to be impregnated with chloroform and wrapped round the head of the sentry, Stoyan.'

For a long time the accused said nothing.

'Well, speak!' said the magistrate.

'Not a drop of my chloroform was used that night,' the accused said. 'Not a drop. There is a graduated scale on the bottle and I know the level of the liquid. It was exactly the same as it is now."

'Could anyone confirm that?' asked the magistrate.

The accused shrugged, then he gave a little laugh.

'You know,' he said, 'this business with my towel really is intriguing, and that of my fingerprints even more so. If you're any good at your job, no doubt you will arrive at the true explanation, but if you keep on wasting your time with my humble person you'll never arrive at the truth.'

'At the moment, the truth seems to be bound up with your humble person,' retorted the magistrate.

After a short pause, the accused said, 'I have no fears for myself, because I have taken no part in this obscure affair and those investigating it are bound to discover that fact. These days, I am quite sure, it is just not possible for a person to be condemned for a crime he has not committed. I am quite confident of the outcome.'

That concluded the third examination.

Colonel Manov observed that Metodi Parashkevov appeared not to appreciate his position, that he had a noose round his neck and one foot on the scaffold, so to speak. Such guilelessness was admirable and pathetic. It was splendid that a man sure of his innocence could be so calm and untroubled; pathetic that he could not see the danger he was in, but was so optimistically sure of the outcome despite the evidence that had accumulated against him: premeditated assault on a sentry; breaking into a military post, theft of a top secret document—'you know the penalty that that carries!' wrote Manov. 'That the case has not gone to the court is due not to lack of proof, but to the slowness of our bureaucracy. I have indicated our desire to try and get to the bottom of this affair and find out its ramifications and who is really behind it, and that it would be desirable that Metodi Parashkevov should remain available for us, but obviously we cannot have unlimited time, and if we don't discover anything more within a reasonable period, the case will have to be proceeded with and justice, as they see it, done.

'As far as this Department's own measures go, apart from your own mission, sections of the frontier on either side of Momchilovo are being closely guarded, and it seems improbable that the map can have been smuggled across, if that is its destination. We have no report of any unauthorized attempt to approach the frontier. This still does not mean that the map is not in the hands of some foreign agent.

'The messages sent by the clandestine transmitter came from an area to the north-north-west of Momchilovo, approximately twelve miles from the village. On one occasion, at the time of the second transmission, a plane was circling in the area at a height of 20,000 feet, but had gone higher and flown off in an unknown direction before our interceptors could take off. It may have been present on the occasion of the first transmission, for at that time only a visual watch was being kept and it was not spotted.

'Keep in touch with the police at Smolyan; remember you're in the area as an archaeologist; be prudent and don't go off by yourself without being armed.

'You will by now have your portable transmitter and we shall keep radio watch for any signal from you at the time and on the wavelengths given on the attached sheet.'

With this report came further minor details about the geologists and life histories of the service members of the survey at Momchilovo.

The sky had clouded over and it looked as though the day was going to turn to rain. Zakhov went indoors and up to his room to wait for the car that was going to take him to Momchilovo.

10

THERE WERE two inns in Momchilovo. The larger, which was also the newer, had a large metal signboard above the door on which was painted in large bold letters RESTAURANT KARABAIR. The restaurant, to use the title it gave itself, occupied the entire ground floor of the building, the rest of which was taken up by the offices of the Momchilovo and Area Cooperative. The restaurant had large windows that looked out onto the shapeless open space known as 'the square'; it was very clean, had white cloths on the tables and vases of artificial flowers, and behind the zinc counter of the bar were rows and rows of shelves sparsely filled with bottles. The people of Momchilovo were very proud of their 'restaurant' and liked to go there for a liqueur and to listen to the wireless. Some were secretly embarrassed by the white tablecloths and polished parquet floor and would have much preferred scrubbed boards on which to stamp their hobnailed boots. As it was, they had to repress all such exhibitions of enthusiasm or delight and behave like the 'cultured' people they were expected to be.

The three teachers of the local school, the bookkeeper of the Agricultural Co-operative, and the head of the Survey, Colonel Injov, all lunched at the restaurant which at that hour would have been empty but for them. In the evening, however, their numbers were swollen by the presence of the young agricultural officer and his wife, who was always smiling happily and wore a yellow everlasting flower behind her ear.

The other establishment, the old inn, was on the eastern fringe of the village at the junction of the two roads, that from Lakité and the main one through the village. It was a low, one-storeyed building of venerable age. The paint on its front was peeling; there was only one window on the outside, and that heavily barred. You entered up four stone steps and through a narrow door with a slate porch. There was no signboard, just the few letters that time and the weather had not effaced of a painted inscription that once had proclaimed that spirits and tobacco were permitted to be sold within. Below this, where the name of the innkeeper would have figured in the old days, was a broad strip of relatively new red paint, because the inn was now the property of the community and run by it as a public service.

Locally the tavern was known as 'Ilcho's Tavern' or just 'Ilcho's'. Inside it was austere rather than comfortable, but full of atmosphere. It was more spacious than appeared from the outside, with room for a dozen or so tables of scrubbed oak eight or nine feet apart. The floor was the hard trodden earth and the ceiling a criss-cross of great blackened beams. A wooden bar counter stood against the wall opposite the entrance, slightly to the right of it. On the left, in the corner, was an ancient fireplace with a chimney-hook and all the rest of the paraphernalia. The mantelpiece was black with greasy soot, where the smoke had curled up over it on days when the wind was in the wrong direction.

Between the hearth and the counter was a doorway, the door itself having disappeared leaving just the casing and the hinge-pins. This led into an adjoining room, the walls of which were lined with sofas covered with aged but colourful rugs, in the middle of which time had worn faded patches where people sat. In the centre of the room was a long table on short, squat legs. Although it had been there for longer than anyone could remember, it had still not achieved equilibrium on the uneven floor. The room was lighted by an oblong window that looked out onto a crossroads. The inn having been built on an eminence, from this particular window you could see the minaret of the old mosque and a long stretch of the road to Lakité.

The new restaurant, the Karabair, had taken some of Ilcho's customers, either because they felt drawn by the fact that you could sit there listening to the radio and drink beer in the summertime or hot soup in winter, and sample the new-fangled hors d'œuvres that were served if you ordered a glass of expensive spirits, or simply because they wished to be thought modern and progressive, as, for example, did the manager of the flourishing Agricultural Co-operative, who encouraged its members to use the restaurant as their club.

The Karabair and the new school building symbolized progress and the new spirit of the country as far as the people of Momchilovo were concerned, and for a time it looked as if Ilcho's old tavern would be deserted altogether. But it was too much of an institution, and within its walls was an atmosphere of warmth and comradeship that was incompatible with parquet floor and white tablecloths. The older members of the community remained faithful to Ilcho's, as did a few others who disliked having the raucous noise of the radio always buzzing in their ears. They and the odd lumberman from the camp up on the mountains saved the old tavern from having to close down.

Once the people of Momchilovo had satisfied their curiosity about the new restaurant, they came more and more to remember that the great barrels in the cellars at Ilcho's contained wine older, richer and much better than any you were served in Karabair. Also, the taverner, Marco Krumov, who managed the tavern for the rural co-operative, always had under the counter a few demijohns of yellow plum brandy, a fragrant, powerful beverage that brought colour to the cheeks of the aged and caused the eyes of the lumbermen to light up. It truly deserved to be called *eau-de-vie*. Krumov would have none of the Crème de Menthe and other new-fangled drinks that the Karabair offered its clients, and whatever you thought of the Karabair's hors d'œuvres, you had to admit that nothing you got there could equal Ilcho's speciality: baked pimento pickled in oil and vinegar. The Karabair also served pimentos, but you could scarcely taste them, while those you got at Ilcho's were little green flames straight from Hades, so that you needed a tongue lined with a double coating of leather if the strength of them was not to bring tears to your eyes.

Marco Krumov never served soup or prepared dishes. At Ilcho's you ate dried mutton, ham, eggs fried with onion and cheese, or spit-roasted chickens. The menu never varied, but what you got there was so good that no one wished for any innovations.

The two men were as different as the establishments they managed. The manager of the Karabair was dry and unbending, always looking about him as if suspecting something to go or be done wrong; while Marco Krumov was stout and red-cheeked, with the complexion of a young man though he was already in his fifties. He wore a moustache with waxed ends turned up, a fashion popular among young patriots in the days when the country was still ruled by the Turks, and this gave his face a look of alertness and energy that was belied by the evidence of his paunch. His eyes twinkled and were full of laughter, often a little malicious, but it was not easy to remain sad or dispirited in his company. He was a perpetual reminder that the world held pleasures and delights as well as cares and worries. He had grey hair, a fat, pleasant face, huge hairy arms, with the sleeves always rolled up beyond the elbows, and his shirt, which he wore outside his trousers in the old style, would obviously never recover its pristine whiteness.

In the winter the wind whistled and howled in the chimney of the great fireplace, and sometimes a downdraught off the mountains would send a puff of wood ash into the room scarcely less white than the snow falling outside. The fire was always alight and in its hot ashes Krumov roasted the potatoes that accompanied every meal.

When the Geological Survey first came to Momchilovo, its members inevitably patronized the modern Karabair, with its familiar atmosphere of chrome and wax-cloth and blaring wireless. The food there was more 'civilized' and urban than the rustic fare you got at the tavern. But Ilcho's had its clientele too: the schoolmaster, Metodi Parashkevov, went there not regularly, but frequently; old Grozdan, president of the Agricultural Co-operative, still came in, though he considered it his duty to drink his evening anisette in the more 'cultured' atmosphere of the Karabair. At Ilcho's he would never sit down, as though that would be to turn his back on progress and modernity as represented by the Karabair, but had his drink or drinks standing at the bar on the pretext that he was in a hurry and had just looked in for a moment.

Old Grozdan was a true farmer if ever there was one. He was short and stocky, had a red weatherbeaten face and a bald head tanned the colour of old copper. He had chubby cheeks, twinkling eyes and ears that stuck out almost at right-angles from his head just under the sheepskin cap that you never saw him without and which they appeared to support. He had only one real passion in life: growing tobacco; his hobby, if you can call it that, was playing the mediator and trying to reconcile those who had quarrelled or grown to hate each other, for which activities he had earned one or two people's undying ingratitude. He enjoyed a glass of anisette, and now that he was past sixty used to take one before breakfast.

The schoolmaster was a quiet man who seldom had much to say for himself. He drank very moderately, but consumed large quantities of Krumov's pimentos and in return often presented him with a hare or a capercailzie, which the taverner would prepare for his regulars in the old ways, often over an open fire as the insurgents used to do in the days of the Turks, when they had to take to the mountains—and there is no better or tastier way of cooking game. A solemn hush would fall upon the company when such a dish was served, but the schoolmaster's face remained impassive and he would eat only the most modest share.

Another regular was the vet. It was not easy to see what brought this quiet, rather timid, inoffensive creature to the rustic tavern, when you would have expected him to have gone with the others to the restaurant. It was an unexpected sign of individuality and made you feel that perhaps there was more to the vet than you had supposed.

The actual turning-point in the tavern's fortunes was when the schoolmaster brought Boyan Icherenski, the chief geologist, to sample a jugged hare he had shot. Icherenski was one of those gourmands who consider themselves gourmets, and he ate very nearly half the hare himself, wiping up quantities of gravy with huge pieces of bread. It was a true compliment to Krumov's skill as a cook, and though he appreciated it, the others did not, for they went short.

Having cleaned his plate and polished off a litre of the tavern's truly excellent wine, Boyan Icherenski undid a button or two and, leaning back, looked round the smaller room in which the meal had been served.

'What a splendid lair you have here,' he said, and laughed. 'And to think that I have been lodging within a stone's throw of such a place and never knew of its existence. How could you let me go to the Karabair all this time, Parashkevov! I can scarcely forgive you.'

The schoolmaster smiled delightedly and Krumov brought another bottle and placed it on the table before Icherenski. 'On the house,' he said. After that Icherenski swore that he would never eat anywhere in Momchilovo but at Ilcho's.

Boyan Icherenski was big without being tall. He had a powerful head, a great bull neck, and arms and fists that any woodman would have envied. He had a high forehead, protruding cheekbones and a strong, square jaw. It was a striking face, and the most striking thing about it was the colour of the eyes: they glowed almost yellow when he was irritated or in high spirits, and when tired or pensive they were almost chestnut.

He had a clear speaking voice with a tone of great warmth. His movements were gentle and his step surprisingly light for someone of his bulk. He had the gift of imparting gaiety, although he seldom laughed himself. When in his company most people felt stimulated and gay and needed little encouragement to burst into song, but somehow Icherenski never added his voice to theirs. There was a natural reticence about him, or maybe it was just diffidence. Perhaps it was because of this that he was always most reluctant to talk about himself, though he had things to his credit of which most people in his position would have been only too glad to boast. He had discovered oil in the basin of the Maritza and at the foot of the wooded flanks of Stranga, both finds of considerable importance. If he liked you, no one could be more pleasant than Boyan Icherenski; but he had an extraordinarily aloof manner with those he disliked or thought of no account and, if he had to address them, did so without looking at them, his eyes as unseeing as if the space where they stood had been empty.

Because of this people did not readily ask him questions, least of all intimate ones, and thus no one knew what everyone was dying to find out, why his wife lived in Plovdiv, forty miles beyond Smolyan which was itself a good hour's drive away, instead of in Momchilovo, where there was ample room for her and any family she might have. As it was, every Saturday afternoon Boyan Icherenski mounted his motorcycle and rode off down the execrable road to Smolyan, returning late on Monday morning to the constant irritation of Colonel Injov, head of the Survey.

The day following Icherenski's introduction to Ilcho's he returned bringing with him two other members of the Survey: Captain Kaludiev and Kuzman Christoforov, a mining engineer; and after that there was no doubt that life had really returned to the old tavern. Every day at noon and again in the evening, the three members of the Survey (at least), the schoolmaster and the shy, diffident little vet, gathered round the low oval table in the rear room.

Now that the tavern enjoyed such distinguished patronage, old Grozdan let himself be tempted, and gave up the pretence of being in too much of a hurry to sit down. Now, especially in the evenings, you could see his broad, straight back, leaning slightly forward, as he rested his forearms on the table. It was only too obvious that the old man felt much more at ease in the tavern with its blackened beams and earthen floor than in the parquet-and-chrome smartness of the restaurant. At Ilcho's he allowed himself to relax and after a glass or two he would forget his dignity as president of the Agricultural Co-operative and acknowledged expert on tobacco growing, and sing. He was a born singer and, had he been trained as a young man, he might have made a name for himself. His songs were the old, old songs of the Rhodopes, which are claimed to have originated with Orpheus who at one time lived among those humpy hills, charming all the animals as he did elsewhere. However that may be, there is a beauty to the songs of the Rhodopes, both to the words and the melody, which transcends those of ordinary folk song and sets them apart.

The only person who appeared immune to the spell of the atmosphere at Ilcho's was Colonel Injov, head of the Survey. He used to go there but only because he considered it his duty to know where his subordinates went and to see how they behaved. He would even sit down, or perhaps it would be more accurate to say that he perched briefly on the end of the sofa and Krumov would bring him a glass of brandy and honey on a tiny wooden tray, after which the severity of his expression might relax a little, but he never allowed himself to relax properly or even to stay long. He was, and had to remain, the C.O.

Stefan Injov was a bachelor in his fifties, lean, bald, rather round-shouldered, with an aquiline nose and thin, bluish lips. He was always impeccably neat, clean-shaven and kept his boots most beautifully polished. He was strict and never seemed satisfied, so that his subordinates rather feared him and the villagers had a great respect for him. The men, all of whom had been in the army at one time or another, always gave him a military salute. You seldom heard him laugh, and when he smiled it gave his face a sad look as if he were ill or exhausted. He did not drink, but he smoked continuously and, if ever things went wrong, the two glass ashtrays on his desk would overflow with cigarette-ends and the files and papers be covered with a layer of ash, as if a volcano had erupted.

He was coldly polite to everyone. He could be pleasant in a reserved sort of way or, when annoyed, bitingly sarcastic. He was a solitary person, never seeking the company of the others, who never seemed to seek his either.

Some ten days after the assault on the sentry at Iliazov's and the arrest of the schoolmaster had set tongues buzzing and brains reeling with speculation, the usual company was assembled in the back room having an aperitif and waiting for Krumov to produce the fried eggs he had promised them for their midday meal. Even Colonel Injov was there, sitting on the edge of the sofa, sipping his drink and listening to the young vet who, his face flushed with triumph, his diffidence overcome, was telling them all how one of the Agricultural Co-operative's cows, a beast that apparently went by the name of Rashka, had given a yield of milk that was a record not only for the area but probably for the entire country, and how this was due to a new diet he had devised and would now use on the other cows, so that soon Momchilovo would have the best milking record in the country. Old Grozdan growled approvingly, and even Colonel Injov unbent sufficiently to raise his glass to the young man and offer his congratulations. All at once the blare of a motor-horn on the road outside made everyone stop talking and prick their ears in rigid silence.

Momchilovo is not exactly the hub of the world, and the arrival of a car there was an event like that of the monthly mail steamer in a southern archipelago. There were no cars in Momchilovo itself, just the Agricultural Co-operative's truck, and everyone knew the sound of its horn and engine. This was different. It could only be a visitor. An inspector? The thought set everyone wondering: have I done anything wrong? Slipped up over something?

Boyan Icherenski stood up and looked out of the window through which you could see the crossroads and a long stretch of road.

'It's one of the Administration's cars from Smolyan,' he said, as he sat down again and took another piece of bread. 'I remember the number.'

Old Grozdan scratched the back of his neck.

'It's probably the Agricultural Officer,' he said, his face looking old and worried.

Other suggestions were made, but then Krumov's voice was heard booming by the door.

'Come in, comrades. Come in!'

11

Two MEN were standing on the threshold of the tavern: one, the Secretary of the Administrative Council in Smolyan, was known to most of those whose heads were now craning round the doorway that led into the back room. The other, taller, thinner, younger, was a stranger to them all. There was a certain urban elegance about his grey suit and his choice of tie—and the way it was tied showed him to be a man of some taste who gave thought to his clothes. For once Zakhov had repressed his love of dressing up and disguise and was not even acting a part, but just being himself; thus no one recognized in this elegant visitor from the distant world of the city the slightly hunchbacked mechanic who had come to Momchilovo on a motorcycle a fortnight before.

The Secretary of the Administrative Council announced that he was in a great hurry and could not accept the immediate invitation to stay for lunch. However, he agreed to a glass of wine, which he drank standing while, briefly, he introduced the other and explained why he had brought him. The stranger's name, he told them, was Avakum Zakhov and he was a historian and archaeologist whom the Academy of Sciences in Sofia had asked to study the ancient history of the southern Rhodopes. As a preliminary he had come to Momchilovo as a convenient centre from which to familiarize himself with the

Karabair area and its surroundings. He hoped, he said, that they would give him all the help in their power and any information they might have. He then drained his glass, wished Zakhov a pleasant and profitable stay in Momchilovo, and, with a 'Good day, Comrades' that embraced them all, he turned and went out. Shortly afterwards they heard the car start up and drive off.

Boyan Icherenski, who appeared to consider himself appointed the spokesman, invited the new arrival to join them and called to the taverner for more wine and another place. He then introduced each of them individually, giving their names and the essential details about them: Grozdan, President of the Agricultural Co-operative and provider of the daily bread; Kuzman Naumov Christoforov, mining engineer with the Geological Survey; Captain Kaludiev, also with the Survey when not courting the lady doctor; and the young vet. Zakhov shook hands with each in turn across the table. Then Krumov placed a plate of fried eggs and sausage in front of him and, taking a large piece of bread, he fell to with excellent appetite.

All the while old Grozdan had kept his eyes fixed on the newcomer, and every now and again scratched the back of his head. His brow was furrowed in puzzlement and the effort of thought.

'I believe we've had a letter about you,' he said at length. 'At least, we had a letter quite recently: yesterday or the day before. It was from the Academy of Something-or-other in the capital, asking us to provide facilities, whatever that means, for someone they were sending somewhere; but blow me if I can remember if they mentioned a name.'

The old man felt in his several pockets in turn, while Zakhov watched him, a smile of amusement hovering round his mouth.

'No. I must have shoved it in the drawer,' the old man announced. 'What did you say his name was?' he added, turning to Icherenski.

'Zakhov, Avakum Zakhov,' Zakhov said.

'Ah well. I expect that was it,' Grozdan muttered and tapped his glass as a sign for Krumov to fill it up.

Having cleaned his plate neatly with a piece of bread and popped it into his mouth, Zakhov put his hand into his trouser pocket as though about to pay the taverner for his meal, but Icherenski, with the lordly gesture of a *grand seigneur* of the old days, told Krumov to charge the other's lunch to him. Zakhov thanked him and bowed across the table, then, turning to Krumov, said, 'And for my account, please, a glass of this excellent wine for everyone here, including yourself.' Krumov hitched his trousers up, made a half-hearted attempt to tuck his great belly in at the top, and went to fetch a fresh bottle.

Then came the question of quarters: where was Zakhov to stay? Neither the tavern nor the restaurant had proper guest-rooms, and the members of the Survey all lived out in lodgings in various houses in the village. Old Grozdan, whose duty it was to see visitors housed, hummed and hawed. Of course, there were quite a number of comfortable rooms in the village, but they were really all let to the schoolteachers and the members of the Survey. It wouldn't be easy to get the new arrival anything as nice. One gathered that the old man had not taken an immediate liking to the archaeologist.

'He could have a bed in my dispensary until you can find him something better,' the young vet suggested.

'That would help,' Icherenski said.

Zakhov sighed and spread out his hands in a gesture of apology.

'I must confess to being abominably squeamish,' he said. 'The sight of a sick animal makes me feel quite ill, I am afraid. And you only have to point a syringe at me and I feel faint. I scarcely think those are the lodgings for me.'

Grozdan looked at him in open-mouthed astonishment.

What urban sentimentality! Anyway, if an animal was ill, you helped it. Then he was heard to mutter, 'Damn city fool,' or something that sounded very like it. If Zakhov heard it, he paid no attention to the remark.

'Injections don't worry me, I must say,' said Captain Kaludiev, and he added, 'Perhaps because I like shooting Cupid's arrows myself. Anyway, I have a big room that faces south and you are welcome to share it for a while, if you like.'

Kaludiev, an artillery captain, who looked like a Greek athlete of antiquity, was a great and obvious womanizer, at that time laying seige to the district's doctor, Nadia Nacheva.

'You're very kind,' Zakhov said. 'The flat of my dreams will have windows looking south, a bathroom with a shower, lavatory and bidet, but I'm such a light sleeper the least thing wakes me up, and as for snores . . .'

Grozdan grunted with impatient exasperation.

'I happen not to snore,' Christoforov said in a cold tone of voice, for which there seemed no justification, yet it cast a chill on the company.

That he had even made the offer was remarkable, for normally he was grim and unapproachable. Christoforov was tall, rather thin, with prematurely grey hair and cold ash-grey eyes that gave the impression of seeing everything and yet perceiving nothing. His clothes were of excellent cut, yet he never brushed or pressed them or took proper care of them. His shoes were obviously expensive, yet never polished; his shirts were of fine poplin, imported, but rarely clean. He was broad-shouldered and quite muscular. He looked forceful, yet his movements were heavy and aimless. There was a dull resonance to his voice, almost as if his vocal chords were artificial. For half a minute no one spoke.

Zakhov broke the silence.

'Thank you for the offer—at least, I suppose it was an offer?' he said. 'I would love to live with a mining engineer, but I'm horribly afraid you may talk in your sleep, and I really dare not accept.'

'As you wish,' Christoforov replied and poured himself out another glass, while they all sat in silence again.

'You obviously like your comfort,' old Grozdan remarked at length. 'There is a room, a very comfortable one and big enough for three people—on the first floor, so there's no one to disturb you.'

'You mean Mrs Balavanova's?' Captain Kaludiev said and winked at Zakhov. 'She's a fine piece.'

'What? You too?' Icherenski exclaimed and, picking up a piece of bread, he crumbled it angry between his fingers, while Zakhov watched him intently.

Icherenski's anger was not with Captain Kaludiev, but with Grozdan. The old man's face took on the expression of one who has made an unpardonable gaffe. He opened his mouth, as if to say something, but shut it again and lowered his gaze to the table.

Kaludiev gave a whistle and looked out of the window.

'What's all this?' Zakhov said. 'Is the room already occupied, promised or what?'

They all looked at each other. It was left to Icherenski to answer the question. He gave a little cough and then said, 'It is, perhaps, a rather delicate matter. The room is, indeed, comfortable——'

'And Mrs Balabanova is indeed attractive,' Captain Kaludiev put in, with a naughty wink.

'Such a remark is quite out of place!' Icherenski said severely. Then, after a pause, he turned to Zakhov and went on. 'The thing is that it has a tenant, though at the moment he is not here and we do not know when or even if he will return.'

He then went on to tell Zakhov briefly of the great affair that occupied so much of all their thoughts; how the local schoolmaster, Metodi Parashkevov, had been arrested and was now in prison accused of assault, breaking in, theft of secret documents and the rest of it.

'If he's done all that,' Zakhov said, 'I should think I could safely have the room. He's not going to come back, is he?' and he made a rather inelegant gesture of tightening a noose round his neck.

They all looked at him wide-eyed. Old Grozdan's face was a study, dislike and contempt struggling to overcome his inbred awe of city folk. A disdainful smile had appeared on Christoforov's lips. Icherenski blew his nose noisily.

'He'll be hanged, surely?' Zakhov went on; then, lighting a cigarette, he leaned back comfortably against the wall and let his gaze travel from one to the other, an enigmatic half-smile on his lips.

'Actually, I was told about this business on my way here. I gather he's made a full confession.'

'Confession? That's peculiar,' Icherenski said and old Grozdan sighed so deeply it might have been he who was due for hanging, and not the schoolmaster.

'My God, what a revolting little beast,' Kaludiev exclaimed and dealt the table such a blow with his fist that Christoforov's glass fell over, spilling half its contents into his lap. Christoforov did not move, nor did his expression change. 'I always said you should mistrust a man who can't laugh and who doesn't like female company,' Kaludiev said sententiously.

'Well, it's my good fortune,' Zakhov said. Then he laughed and went on, 'You know, about six months ago I was working on a dig at Nicopolis and Istrum and an old gipsy woman told my fortune—using haricot beans, incidentally. "My young man," she said, "you were born under a favourable star, which rises into the sky when the grapes are ripening and the maize harvest is at hand. All that you undertake at that season will succeed." I'm sure she was right. These old gipsy women do have strange powers at times. And here we are: autumn is at hand, the grapes are nearly ripe and the maize is ready to harvest. My star is in its ascendant.'

'You and I will get on well,' Captain Kaludiev said out of the blue, and filling Zakhov's glass and his own, he leaned across the table and planted a resounding kiss on the archaeologist's left cheek. Zakhov returned the noisy salutation, the two men clinked glasses and drained them in one draught.

'All the same,' Icherenski said, a smile showing that he had recovered his good humour, 'I wouldn't advise you to live there. At least, I wouldn't like to sleep in the room of a man who had been hanged.'

'Do I look as if I would be frightened of ghosts?' Zakhov demanded.

They had to admit that he didn't. Anyway, Parashkevov hadn't been hanged—yet.

Then Icherenski stood up and said that it was time for him to get back to his office—as indeed it was for everyone—and with a farewell wave of his hand he walked towards the door.

'Hallo, there! You've forgotten to pay,' Zakhov called.

The young vet shuddered at such effrontery. How dare he —to someone of Icherenski's standing and seniority? But, evidently, Zakhov knew men and how to deal with them, for Icherenski just turned and, smiling, said, 'It's not the end of the month yet. I settle my bill here on the first of every month. Your lunch will be included, never fear!'

'That's all I want to know,' Zakhov said. 'You can include as many others as you like,' he added with a laugh.

Icherenski waved his arm, and walked out. Just as he disappeared through the doorway, Zakhov jumped to his feet and ran after him.

'Show me which house this room's in,' he said.

Icherenski's face clouded, but then brightened again, and raising his arm he pointed and said, 'You can see it from here. The third house on the left. That one with a brick part wall.'

'Ah, yes. I see.'

'Anyway, I shall take you there and make the arrangements,' growled old Grozdan, his face set and rather sullen. 'Anna Balabanova would not take you in unless someone from the Council introduced you.' Then he slapped his sheepskin cap onto his head.

'These your things?' he said, pointing to the two bags standing beside the door. Zakhov nodded and the old man picked one up and walked off with it as effortlessly as if he had been empty-handed. Zakhov took hold of the other and hurried after him. The downward tilt to his shoulder and the fact that his left arm stuck out from the side showed how heavy the case was. He had to run a few awkward, bent-kneed steps to catch the old man up.

12

ANNA BALABANOVA was in her thirties, but she had not yet begun to look her age. She was tallish for a woman, with a shapely bust, long legs and a small waist. Her mouth was, perhaps, on the small side and her eyes were usually rather sad and had a liquid quality about them that went straight to your heart. She was a widow. Her husband had been manager of the sheep farm that formed part of the Agricultural Co-operative. He had had a heart-attack and died five years previously when they had been married a relatively short time. There were no children. Balabanov had been considerably older than his wife and the envy of the women neighbours attributed part, if not all, of the blame for his sudden demise to her demands on his physical companionship, which, they would say, dropping their voices, had been 'insatiable'. But what married woman without children is not the target of envious female tongues? The only person able to tell you how much truth there was in this accusation was no longer able to give evidence, so let us leave it at that.

The thing that really annoyed her female neighbours most was that though men obviously found her attractive and though, equally obviously, she was not indifferent to their attentions, she was in no hurry to remarry. Old Balabanov had left her a good house and sufficient revenue from his flocks for her not to need a husband to help her keep it going, and she had no responsibilities beyond her job, which she took very seriously and which she did very well. In fact, she was rapidly becoming esteemed as the local sheep expert, and it was expected that when the temporary manager went back to the State farm from which he had been posted she would be appointed in his place. That she should have been so efficient and clever, as well as having the youthful looks and sex appeal the others all envied, only made matters worse. Thus, those wanting to know the truth about Anna Balabanova had best not ask her neighbours, from whom they would hear many references to a rabbit-skin waistcoat and coat of fox fur and men in general and the local schoolmaster in particular.

When old Grozdan and Avakum Zakhov reached the house with the brick part wall and entered the courtyard, they saw that the door was open, so presumably Anna Balabanova was at home. They went up to the open door and halted. Zakhov's arm was aching from carrying his heavy hold-all, which he now put down, rubbing his aching muscles with his other hand, but old Grozdan seemed unaware that he was holding anything and made no attempt to rest the heavy case on the ground. Through the open doorway they could see an almost girlish figure squatting beside a huge copper cauldron, which she was busy polishing. The woman had her back to them and was humming to herself, so that Grozdan had to cough twice before she heard them and leaped lightly and easily to her feet. Turning to look at them, she smoothed the front of her black woollen skirt and her face lit up with a smile.

Zakhov noted with approval that her hair was raven black. The energy of her polishing had shaken a long curly wisp onto her face and this she now brushed back with a graceful gesture, using the back of her wrist. And Zakhov was aware of stirrings, and an inner voice counselled him to beware. In his heart of hearts Zakhov, citizen of a modern Communist state, considered himself a Knight of the Round Table manqué. His heart was filled with romantic chivalry, and it did not take much to bring him hurrying, armed cap-à-pie, to the succour of any damsel—or widow?—in need of protection or consolation. That Anna Balabanova was in need of neither the one nor the other was beside the point and made no difference to his readiness to offer them.

Old Grozdan, feeling that so far he had played the part incumbent on the President of the Co-operative and local boss, now said in a gruff, severe tone of voice, 'Why aren't you at work?'

'That's a fine greeting, I must say!' Anna Balabanova said with a little laugh and a sideways glance at Zakhov. 'Good day to you, Father Grozdan. I'm not at work, because I'm on the second shift this week. But come in, won't you?' And she stepped aside to let them pass.

'Put your things down here by the door,' she said, and bending down with an ease that Zakhov envied, she drew out a couple of stools and placed them beside the hearth, gesturing to the two men to be seated. Then she stood, one shoulder against the chimney-breast, head slightly down-tilted to look at them, while old Grozdan gruffly explained who Zakhov was and the nature of their errand. At the mention of Metodi

Parashkevov her eyes misted and the light seemed to drain from her face, and it was a long time before she again looked at Zakhov. Old Grozdan's gruff voice rumbled on, but there was a note of tenderness in it now.

'You must just stack the schoolmaster's things along the wall,' Grozdan said. 'Comrade Zakhov will see they don't come to any harm, and there's no likelihood of Metodi Parashkevov coming back—yet awhile,' he added. 'At least, not while Comrade Zakhov's with us.'

Then the old man got stiffly to his feet and said that he must be getting back to his duties, so they had better just go up.

It was all Zakhov could do to keep his jubilation from showing in his face. Luck was with him, indeed! He could scarcely have hoped to find himself using the schoolmaster's room. Now he would be able to examine it, the house itself, the surroundings, everything about it at leisure and with every right to be there at all times of the day and night. He could have kissed the old man—and Anna Balabanova—but he felt that they would think that was not the right way for an archaeologist to behave, so he had to content himself with rubbing his hands as he looked round the room.

It was a long, low room, a kitchen-cum-living-room such as you find in most old farmhouses in those parts, or used to. That prosperity had recently come to the owner was evident in the flagstones on the floor and the fact that there now was a wooden staircase at one end instead of the ladder that had formerly been the only means of access to the upper floor. Picking up Zakhov's baggage as they passed the outer door, they now followed Anna Balabanova outside into the yard and up an outer staircase that led to a narrow gallery along the back of the house, where it faced a large orchard. Two doors led off the gallery. They were painted, but the paint was old and peeling and there was a faint air of general neglect about this side of the house that contrasted strangely with the well-kept, prosperous appearance of the courtyard and ground floor. Across the two doors ran diagonal cords with great seals on them and Anna Balabanova gestured mutely at them. The old man paused and scratched the back of his neck. Had he the authority to break the seals, or should he send for another member of the Council? Finally he decided that, as President of the Co-operative, he did have the requisite authority, and anyway he had no more time to waste on this cocksure intruder from the outside world, so, with a brusque, determined gesture, he tore the seals down and flung the door open.

'There you are,' he said to Zakhov. 'Mrs. Balabanova will look after you.' Then he turned and a moment later his sheepskin cap disappeared below the level of the first step and they heard his heavy tread as he stomped down the wooden stairs.

Zakhov looked at Anna Balabanova, who with a vague gesture invited him to enter and stepped inside.

The room was a great surprise, so much poorer and barer than he had imagined, even after hearing Kovachev's description of it. Along the wall facing one window was a very ordinary, village-made chest-of-drawers; a rather high shelf loaded with books; a big stout table covered with ordinary brown paper, two chairs, a bed and—that was all. On the wall above the bed hung a double-barreled shotgun and a leather cartridge-bag. On the table was a big, shiny microscope plus two racks for test-tubes. There were a spirit lamp, pincers, geological hammers and various bottles of acids and other things. All as described in Captain Kovachev's report.

Anna Balabanova had followed him into the room. Her arm described a circular gesture, as she said, 'It's only the bed, the covers and the chest-of-drawers that belong to me. Everything else is the schoolmaster's. It's all listed in an inventory that I've signed, and if anything is lost or damaged, I shall be held responsible.'

'You've no need to worry,' Zakhov said. 'As you can see, I

have very few clothes and they can perfectly well stay in my case, so don't bother to empty the chest-of-drawers. And as to the other things, I shan't touch them. Please, don't worry on that score.'

Anna Balabanova seemed very quiet and subdued as she put clean sheets on the bed, and Zakhov wondered just how close was the relationship between the schoolmaster and his landlady. And he felt a little stab of jealousy and disappointment. If you can't have a holiday with a young laboratory assistant because duty calls you elsewhere, it would be only just if Fate were to repay you by . . . he would not let himself complete the thought, but walked over to the window and looked out. Away at the limit of vision he could just see the fringe of some fearfully rough, hilly ground which, he realized, must be the fringe of the Zmeitza.

Then he walked out onto the gallery and opened the second of the two doors. This led into a much smaller room, a real junkroom full of old books, newspapers, journals, stuffed birds and animals—squirrel, capercailzie—heavens, even a small bear! The bear stood on a wooden stand balanced, rather precariously he thought, on a long packing-case. There was a rather rickety-looking shelf on which stood a number of dirty bottles with specimens in alcohol—or was it formalin? One had a coiled-up snake with a whitish belly and a speckled band that was quite new to him. In other jars were lizards and salamanders and several creatures he could not begin to identify. A stuffed weasel with glass eyes veiled by cobwebs was looking out of the one window, a small, heavily barred rectangle that had not been cleaned for many a year.

All at once Zakhov felt that he was being watched and, turning round slowly, saw Anna Balabanova standing behind him.

'Most of this is the schoolmaster's, too,' she said. 'The books, specimens and, well, most of the things here. He stuffed animals and other things to show to the schoolchildren. He is a good, kind man,' she said, and there was a momentary choke in her voice. 'And a very good schoolmaster,' she went on. 'These things have not been inventoried. One day I must clear it all out, or at least tidy it up. I'm ashamed you should have seen it like this, but I haven't even looked in here for a year or more. It could make a nice room for someone. It's not too big for me to weave a rug for it.'

Then she turned and looked at him, and it seemed to him that away at the back of her eyes was a dawning sparkle of light and laughter.

'Are you married?' she asked.

'I'm the father of six,' he said jocularly. (But that scarcely answered her question.)

'Poor you,' she said, and there seemed to be a smile hovering round her lips. Then she looked up into his face. 'Now I must go up to the farm and see to my sheep. I shan't be back until the evening, so if you go out please lock up. Here are your keys.' She turned and walked slowly down the stairs.

'Thank you,' he said. 'I shall look forward to this evening.' And at once he thought, I shouldn't have said that. I mustn't get involved.

13

ZAKHOV gave his landlady ten minutes to get out of the house and be sure that she wasn't coming back because she had forgotten something, then he went down and began examining the outside of the house.

Between the south wall at the back of the house and the big

orchard grew a gnarled old pine tree. Its crest was about level with the eaves and two big, thick branches reached out towards the house, almost touching the rail of the gallery. In fact, at one time they must have been almost in at the window, for they had been lopped, leaving blunt ends a good two inches across.

That would be one way of getting in uninvited, Zakhov thought as he looked up at the branches, which were stout enough to bear a man's weight.

Beyond the tree was the orchard, which had obviously been let run more or less wild, evidence of the lack of a man in the household. The trees were mostly plums, and they stood knee-deep in grass that was dry and almost yellow. Beyond them was a fence. The distance between the old pine and this fence was, he judged, a good thirty yards, perhaps more. He paced it, and found it to be thirty-three paces. The fence was not high and he had no difficulty in seeing over it. On the other side was a narrow track. Wheelmarks showed that it was used by ox-carts, for which, judging by the tracks, there was only just enough room. The track zig-zagged between the back hedges of the cluster of houses there, but he could not see where it led.

A path ran obliquely from one side of the house to a cluster of low buildings half-way down one side of the orchard. These proved to be a pig-sty without pigs, a stable that had ceased even to smell of horses and, above it, a hayloft with a roof of black, mouldering thatch that had partly fallen in. There was an open shed, the only one of the buildings which showed signs of being used, for inside there was a good big pile of wood and a chopping block with an axe stuck in it. The axe was not rusty.

There appeared to be nothing else in the garden.

Returning to the gnarled pine, Zakhov began scrutinizing the ground at its foot, especially that on the side of the orchard.

There was a grim smile on his face as, bent almost double, he slowly made his way from the tree to the back fence. Here and there he could see grasses that were more yellow and withered than others. Obviously they had been trampled before nature started to wither them.

These tiny signs led Zakhov to near the fence, but the last few inches of ground were covered with brambles. A man could easily have straddled them and at the same time got a leg across the fence; but a woman would have had to pull up her skirt and either put a foot on the brambles or dig a toe into the fence on the other side. He could see no signs of any such thing. It was most likely that whoever had come this way, as someone had and probably more than once, had been a man. Obviously it was not a short cut in regular use by the inhabitants of the house; so, who was the visitor? Legitimate or otherwise? Could he be some moustached village Romeo paying the pretty widow a clandestine visit? If so, then the tracks should continue beyond the pine to the back door under the gallery, which, from where he stood had all the appearance of never being used. He found that they did not. The tracks stopped at the tree. That told its own tale.

Running up the outside stairs again, Zakhov went into the schoolmaster's room. As he had hoped, he found the window-hooks hanging straight down, not in their staples. They were rusty. He gave the window a push; it did not move; he pushed a little harder and with a creak the two halves opened. The gallery was too narrow for them to go back flat against the wall. The rail caught them when they were at an angle of about eighty degrees. He closed them again and returned to the tree. The only difficult part was between the third and fourth branches, he decided. You would have to give yourself a good hoist up there and hold on tight. He began to climb. Reaching the fourth branch, which had been broken off short a long time before, he put one arm round the trunk in a rather convulsive grip and gingerly got his magnifying glass out of his pocket and began to examine the branch along its short length with the utmost care. His hovering glass halted, rose up a little way, halted again. Then he returned the glass to his pocket; produced a pocket knife, opening a blade with his teeth, and carefully cut off a sliver of bark, slipped it into his pocket and then climbed down.

As he mounted the stairs again, he felt a drop of rain and, looking up, saw a great black cloud about to blot out the sun. Mentally he blessed the schoolmaster for his scientific hobbies and his foresight in acquiring a microscope. Back in his room, he detached a scale from the piece of bark and placed it on the glass under the microscope. A moment later he was staring down at a blue filament, a fibre of blue wool. Lighting a cigarette, Zakhov took a few avid pulls, then he got out his pocket-book, took from it a piece of paper and unfolded it, revealing a few blue fibres. Taking one, he placed it beside the other and compared the two under the lens. They were identical.

Evidently the same gloved hand had held the branch of the old pine as had grasped the bar in the window in Iliazov's house. What was the connection between the two? Even if the schoolmaster had wished to avoid being seen when returning to the house, there could never have been any need for him to climb the tree to gain access to his room. To have done so would have been ridiculous. Who then—or who else—had been climbing the fence and coming through the orchard to climb the tree? Of course, that would not be the only blue woollen glove in the world, though it might be the only one in Momchilovo. But supposing they were made or sold locally? Lots of people might have them. He would have to find out about that.

Feeling quite pleased with his afternoon's work, he next turned his attention to the junk-room. It was not that anything there had caught his attention, but he had a feeling that there was something there that concerned him or at least the case. He stood just inside the doorway and a little to one side, so that the full light flooded in through the doorway, and let his gaze slowly travel round. Ah! That brown bear! None of the other stuffed animals had been moved for ages: their stands were dusty and some were draped with cobweb, but the bear was relatively clean and its stand had been wiped quite recently. Why just the bear?

Zakhov went closer and subjected it to a further scrutiny. Then he gave it a prod with a finger; it rocked. It could not have been stowed away like that; it had been shifted, presumably quite recently. But why? He picked the bear up, inspected it and the stand. Nothing there. Then he noticed that the lid of the case on which the bear had been standing was not properly closed. He opened it and looked inside. It contained a number of bits of stone of different sizes, shapes and colours. Nothing else. One stone was wrapped in paper and tied with red wool. It was lying on top of the other loose stones and when he picked it up, he saw that on the paper was scribbled in pencil:

Zmeitza. 7 August

That date—7 August? That was exactly a fortnight before the attack on Stoyan and the theft of the map. And what was so special about this stone that it had to be wrapped up? Zakhov knew next to nothing about stones, so he let the packet drop back into the box, making a mental note to ask Sofia for a description of leninite and whether it was found in the form of stone or what. Then he shut the lid and put the bear back on top of it. It now stood firm and did not rock. He wondered whether he should have put it back exactly as it was, but decided that it didn't matter.

The rain had stopped and a smell of damp earth, freshly

washed air and pine-tree came in through the open window. When he returned to what was now 'his' room it felt cold and unfriendly, and he shivered.

There was a lot to think over, and for one who liked to lounge in a chair the schoolmaster's two straight-backed, hard-seated horrors did not look inviting, so Zakhov went and lay on the bed and pulled his big raincoat over him. There was something about Boyan Icherenski, he decided, that he did not like. He felt a sneaking sympathy for his wife, Victoria, who lived in Plovdiv and only saw him at the week-end. A little of him would go a long way. He felt that he must find an early opportunity of making the acquaintance of Victoria Icherenski. For a while he lay looking out of the window at the last of the black cloud disappearing over the jagged pinnacles of the Zmeitza, then his eyes closed and he fell asleep.

He woke to hear a door shut down below. Then came the sound of footsteps that he recognized as Anna Balabanova's. Opening his eyes, he discovered that it was dark and he had to light the lamp to see what he was doing.

His raincoat had a series of pockets in the lining, and these he now filled with what he called his 'field equipment': a length of thin, strong rope; a torch and a spare battery for it; an automatic and two spare loaded magazines and a steel jemmy in a leather case, a real burglar's tool guaranteed to get you into or out of anything. When all was ready, he draped the raincoat round his shoulders, shut the windows and went out.

The courtyard was in darkness, the front door shut. Zakhov went up to the door, listened. He could not hear anything. He coughed. Nothing. Then he tapped on the door. The next moment it opened, and in the light that flooded out he saw Anna Balabanova.

'Gracious, it's you,' she exclaimed in a tone of surprise.

'There's no need for you to knock, you just walk in. Come on; don't stand there outside. Come and get warm. I've just lit a fire.'

Indeed, over her shoulders he could see the hearth where leaping, crackling flames were licking round a vertical structure of logs. He sniffed: wood smoke and boiled potatoes, he decided. The smell of the latter made him realize that he was hungry and his mouth watered.

'I was just on the point of going out,' Zakhov said.

'It looks as though it's going to rain again—why not wait and see?' she said. 'Unless you're in a hurry, that is.'

'Grozdan asked me to call and have a drink with him, but we didn't fix any time.'

'Well, then,' she said, 'why not come in?'

She was, no doubt, well aware of the effect she had on Zakhov, and it must have given her a little thrill of triumph to see the well-polished city shoe move across her threshold in response to her suggestion. What she might not have known was that Zakhov was as much attracted by the smell of her potatoes as by the prospect of a little tête-à-tête with a pretty woman, if not more. His archaeological work had taken him into many out-of-the-way parts of the country and he was no stranger to the rustic delights of potatoes with butter and rock salt. At that moment, indeed, he would have sworn there was nothing better.

His second foot followed the first across the widow's threshold and she shut the door behind him. The fire was burning well now and the room full of light and leaping shadows. Zakhov walked across to the hearth and sat down on the low stool beside it and held out his hands. It was only now that he realized how cold he had been.

After a while his hand went to his pocket and pulled out his pipe. He glanced interrogatively at Anna Balabanova, who nodded; so he got out his pouch and filled his pipe and lit it.

'I am just getting my own supper ready,' Anna said, 'nothing much, just potatoes and butter, bread and some cheese, but you are welcome to join me, if you will.'

'I should be very glad to,' Zakhov said and swallowed.

Anna walked away to the back of the room where there was a large dresser. As she busied herself getting things out, Zakhov looked round the room. It was a big room that appeared vast in the firelight. There were shelves on the walls and two copper pots hung from hooks by the door. At the end of one long side was another door. It stood open, but what lay beyond was veiled in blackness. A bedroom, Zakhov thought. Hers, no doubt. Then he remembered seeing a small barred window opposite the tumbledown buildings at the back. The positions corresponded.

Anna came back with plates, knives and forks which she laid on the table. From his low perch, Zakhov saw her from a new angle and suddenly noticed that she was barefoot.

'Aren't you cold?' he said.

'Cold?' she repeated with a puzzled look.

'Yes, walking about barefoot like that.'

'Oh, I see,' and she looked down at her feet, smoothing her skirt back and pulling it up very slightly in a gesture that might —or might not—have been involuntary. Then she gave a gay little laugh. 'Oh, my feet are tough. They're used to it. Good country feet. Don't you ever go barefoot?'

Zakhov blushed and admitted that he didn't. Whether they were tough or not he did not know, but Anna Balabanova had pretty feet and pretty legs too. Zakhov puffed furiously, and with a soft little laugh she turned and went back to the dresser.

Zakhov sat gazing at the fire, his thoughts not very far away. Then her voice came from just behind him.

'Come and eat. It's not much to offer, but I didn't know I was to have company.'

There were potatoes and cheese, a large dish of fried eggs, a huge loaf and a pan of curds.

'Life's a bit empty, when you're a widow,' Anna Balabanova remarked out of the blue, energetically dipping a hunk of bread into the eggs, 'and I'm glad of company. The schoolmaster often used to come in of an evening. He was alone too and didn't really look after himself, so sometimes I used to make a proper meal, a pie, or roast some meat or something like that, but I can't be bothered just for myself. Who could?'

'Not I,' said Zakhov. 'But I love having someone to do it for me.' Then he realized that much more could be read into that remark than he had meant, and he blushed. She, however, did not even look up.

For a while they ate in silence. He wondered how much he dared question her about the schoolmaster. Would she shut up at the first question, or would she be glad to talk about him? He decided there was no harm in trying.

'They say he is a very good schoolmaster,' he said. She nodded. 'He's a bachelor, isn't he? Did he have lots of people coming to see him?'

'Lots of people?' she laughed, throwing back her head. 'No one ever came to see him, that I know of. People all like him, but he's fearfully shy and prefers to keep them at arm's length. He saw people at Ilcho's, but never here. He's a bit of a hermit. Like me.'

'He didn't have any friends?'

'No real friends, no. People liked him, but he never opened up to anyone and so they all remained mere acquaintances.'

'Poor chap,' Zakhov said, and she frowned, as though she did not like the tone of genuine commiseration that had crept into the other's voice, or, at least, did not feel that it was justified. As he looked at her, it struck him that perhaps it wasn't.

'He had a lot in common with one of the game wardens, but he, poor fellow, was eaten by wolves. That was three years ago. They both liked shooting and often went out together; but even so I would hardly call them friends.'

Zakhov felt that it would be wiser not to pursue the subject. He asked her about her job and her face lit up as she told him about the sheep farm and her work there. Proudly she told him how they were now producing twice as much cheese and dairy goods as before up at the farm and so were bound to beat Lakité and the other villages, which meant that there would be a big shareout and they would get a lot of money.

'And what will you do with your money?' Zakhov asked. 'I bet you'll get married.'

She laughed with real amusement.

'If I wanted that, I could find a husband tomorrow,' she said. 'And one that I should like. But that's an easy way out. I want something else, something much more important. My husband was a specialist, an expert sheep-farmer, and I want to become a specialist too. In memory of him. It's work that I like and I do it well. But I need more theoretical knowledge. There's more to it than you might think.' She looked at him and her face was alight and her eyes dancing. 'They've promised to send me on a course in the spring—and that's more important to me than getting married. When I really am a specialist, the farm will be more my home than this house here; but if I'm married, I'll come back here from time to time, so that my poor husband won't get too bored.'

'Would that be the only reason?' Zakhov said with a smile.

'That and to sleep on a box-spring mattress. Have you ever tried one? You don't know you're lying on anything. It's wonderful!'

Then he filled his pipe again and went back to the hearth, while she cleared the table. As Zakhov watched her moving about at the far end of the room, he saw her disappear through the open doorway there, heard a match being struck and a moment later the warm glow of lamplight lit up the scene, at least what he could see of it: the top half of a panel bed and a coverlet of dazzlingly white goatskin; beside it, on the wall, hung a knitted rug. He saw her draw off the coverlet, heard her yawn, saw her arms go out as she stretched, and a sudden gust of wind swept round the house with a moan and a puff of smoke came down the chimney. That's a warning, he told himself.

Slowly he got to his feet. Avakum, he said to himself, all in good time. What is to be, will be—but duty first. He coughed and stepped out in the middle of the room. Anna came towards him.

'Going to old Grozdan?' she said.

'I must,' he said. 'I promised I would.'

'Then, of course, you must. What time is it?'

'After nine.'

She stood there gazing into the fire. The leaping shadows made it impossible to see the expression on her face.

'Good night,' he said and his voice was lower and not nearly so brisk as he meant it to be.

'Do you want to be woken in the morning?' she said suddenly, raising her head and looking him straight in the face.

'No thanks,' he said. 'I think I'll sleep as long as I can. I may be late getting back.'

'You have your key?' she said.

'Yes. The room's locked now. Good night.'

'Good night.'

Zakhov banged the door shut behind him, turned up the collar of his raincoat, as it was raining quite heavily now, and set off down the road that passed the front of the house. It was a dark night and at first he could not make out a thing and had to walk very carefully and slowly. He soon came to where the track led off to the left and turned down it. Thirty paces, he judged, would take him to where someone had been climbing the fence at the bottom of the yard. He counted them carefully, stopped when he reached thirty. Pulling up the skirts of his raincoat, he straddled the fence, swung his leg over and found himself standing in brambles. Carefully freeing his feet, he took a couple of steps forward and found himself knee deep in the long grass.

Now he could just make out the black mass of the house in front of him. The rain hissed in the foliage of the trees and in the dry grass. As he stood there observing and listening, the little barred window in the ground floor that he had judged to be that of Anna's bedroom filled with light and a patch of brightness in which he could see slanting shafts of rain flung onto the wet grass. Quickly a long shadow flitted across it, then all was still.

He moved into the comparative shelter of one of the plum trees and waited. After about ten minutes the light went out and the little window was as black as those above it.

He waited another ten minutes, then walked to the house and taking care to be as quiet as he could—though the sound of the rain would drown all but the loudest noise—he mounted the outside stairs. Reaching the gallery, he paused, quickly unlocked the door of his room and went in.

He had a presentiment that something was going to happen. Perhaps he would have said that he *knew* that something would happen; at all events he lay down on the bed in his clothes. There he lay listening to every sound. He heard the rain stop, or rather the absence of its hiss and patter on the roof told him that it had stopped, and the different, kindlier note of the wind showed that it had abated, though it had not yet died away.

All at once his muscles tensed. He thought he had heard the click of a latch. This was followed by a creak that could have come from hinges, but there was no further click, so either the door—if it was a door—was still open, or it had been closed silently. But which door? It could hardly have been the front door; he would scarcely have heard that even at night. There was a door between the side of the house and the part wall, but that had been wide open and looked as if it were left thus. Perhaps it was shut now? But why? Could it have been shut against him—by someone paying Anna a late visit? Or was its purpose less obvious, more sinister?

The minutes passed and as nothing more happened, his tension relaxed. He had just decided that Anna must have more than the one active admirer and was wondering whether he shouldn't undress and get into bed, when another sound made him catch his breath.

Someone was coming up the stairs. He lay there wide-eyed, rigid. A tread creaked; then there was a long stillness, before he heard the faintest hint of a sound as if a foot was being put down—and again—and again. Now it, or presumably he, was just outside his door. He strained his eyes to see if he could see if the latch moved. Nothing happened. Then came a faint click—but not from his door. It was the latch of the other door, of the junk-room. He dared not sit up, in case the bed creaked; so he lay where he was, every sense alert, willing his ears to hear better. There—that was another click. The door shutting? Yes—because that was the lightest of footsteps on the gallery outside—and now a creak—that same stair-tread as had creaked before.

Now!

Zakhov leapt to his feet, pulled his door open, darted out and, seizing the branches of the pine-tree, swung himself over the rail and let himself be carried towards the ground. He had to drop the last couple of feet, but he retained his balance and set off in pursuit of a dark shape he could see running down the orchard. As he ran, he thrust his hand into his pocket for his electric torch, but just as he pulled it out his foot caught in something and he was flung headlong on his face. As he stumbled to his feet, he realized that it was too late now.

The beam of his torch confirmed that the orchard was empty. He had lost the first round.

He walked back and up to his room, where he undressed and got into bed, cursing himself and wondering why he had not tackled his visitor while he was still in the junk-room. It was some time before he fell asleep.

14

THE NOISE of the wind tearing and tugging at the branches of the old pine woke him. The sun was not yet up. He got up and looked out of the window. Heavy grey clouds were scudding across the sky, but here and there to the south and east were patches of freshly washed blue. I must go and have a look in the junk-room, he thought, but somehow he had no sense of urgency; so first he took his towel and soap and went down to the yard where there was a tap, and there he washed and towelled himself till he was glowing all over. Then he ran upstairs again, shaved and dressed, humming to himself as he did so.

He cleaned his shoes, put on a new pullover, anointed his head with some eau-de-cologne and carefully brushed his hair and surveyed the result in his pocket mirror. Then, at last, he decided to inspect the junk-room.

The gallery and the two doors there had been washed all night by the rain so there was no need to bother to look for prints. He opened the door and looked in; at first glance it looked as if nothing had been moved; slowly he scrutinized each object in turn. Ah! the bear. Wasn't that at a slightly different angle? He was sure it was. You could see a corner of the packing-case that had been hidden before. He picked up the bear and put it on the floor. Then he opened the packing-case: there was the same pile of stones, with the one wrapped in paper on top; the inscription on it was the same: *Zmeitza, 7 August*. Only—it was not the same stone. He remembered perfectly well that the stone he had seen was a strange deep brown, almost chestnut; this was greyish, almost white. Quite different—and rather ordinary.

The sky over the Zmeitza was ablaze as he walked down the wooden stairs for the second time that day. The first rays of the sun were falling straight on the slopes of the Zmeitza, making its crags and fissures stand out more clearly than at any other time of the day. He paused half-way down to look at it. God, what a savage-looking place!

As he turned the corner of the house, he almost banged into Anna Balabanova. She was wearing a short-sleeved embroidered jacket over a deep-cut blouse of some thin material. It made him realize what lovely skin she had.

'I really ought to be up at the farm,' she said. 'Only I overslept. It took me ages to get to sleep. The widow's lot.' She laughed gaily. It was certainly not the laugh of someone whose lot was an unhappy one. Nor, he thought, was the dress that of someone going to work on a sheep farm. As she stood there, hands on her hips, head flung back as she looked up at him, blouse taut across her breasts, he found himself wishing more than ever that it was not on duty that he had come to Momchilovo, or at least that another man's life did not depend on his solving the mystery of Iliazov's house as soon as possible.

'I can imagine occasions when I would not mind taking a long time to get to sleep,' he said. 'So I can't really feel very sorry for you.'

'No, don't feel sorry, please,' she said and in her voice there was a vibrant note—of what? Then she gave another little laugh. 'I must fly,' she said, and she turned and went back indoors.

A minute or two later, he heard the front door open and shut, and she walked off at a brisk pace.

Zakhov's immediate problem was this: was the man who had come upstairs her lover, sent to the junk-room on some really innocent errand and taking care to be quiet merely in order not to disturb the newcomer; or was his visit only to the junk-room and one of which Anna Balabanova was unaware? Or, a third alternative, was the visit nefarious and did she know of it? Was she implicated?

He gave her a minute or two to get well away, then entered the house and went straight to the bedroom at the end of the big living-room. The door was open. The floor, he saw, was of parquet and well polished. Going down on his knees he examined it for the traces of man-sized shoes or boots. There was not a thing to be seen. Either no man had been in there —or he had taken off his shoes before he went in. The floor of the living-room was of earth and there could be no tracks there.

The room was filled with the scent of flowers: of a geranium in a pot that stood on a table, and of muscat grapes that hung round the open window. It was all so innocent and carefree that he could not imagine evil there. On the contrary, there was an idyllic atmosphere that made his mind go back to another summer long years before, when . . .

But there was no time to dwell on that. Going out again, he set off down the road to Ilcho's, where the innkeeper gave him a big plate of *panada* with cheese and some pickled pimentos, which made his mouth burn all morning.

Old Grozdan was just about to pour himself his morning glass of anisette, which he considered the due of those who had passed life's allotted span, when he saw the archaeologist come into his courtyard. He did not like the fellow. His shrewdness told him that he was not altogether what he pretended to be. There were things about him that did not ring true. Was he a rogue—or what? Hurriedly he filled his glass, drained it and, with a sigh of regret, returned the bottle to its cupboard and went towards the door, where his wife was already talking to the meddling fellow. If I had just had my drink five minutes earlier, I would have been on my way to the farm now, he thought. His wife stepped aside, leaving the two men face to face.

'Come in,' said Grozdan. 'Welcome,' he added, rather as an afterthought.

Looking at the archaeologist again, he decided quite definitely that he neither liked nor trusted him. Then his wife hissed at him, 'Remember your manners. You offer a guest a chair.'

Grozdan did so, and they sat down at the far end of the big room, where Grozdan's wife swept a lace cloth over the table and announced that she would bring them a cup of coffee.

It was a big room and full of furniture: a huge wardrobe with double doors; a great solid chest-of-drawers with an alarm clock ticking away on top of it; lace antimacassars on the chairs, pictures on the walls, an enormous panel bed at the other end, little white curtains at the windows. There was so much in it, it made Anna Balabanova's room appear unfurnished.

'You're very comfortable here,' Zakhov remarked, looking round. And to himself he added: but it needs flowers.

'One does what one can,' Grozdan said, a note of pride in his voice.

'You must be doing very nicely,' Zakhov said.

The old man gave his moustache a twirl and glared at Zakhov for this impertinence; but he said nothing. They could hear Grozdan's wife busy in the kitchen. Zakhov pulled out his identity card as an officer of the Counter-Espionage Department and handed it to the old man, who read it, scrutinized the stamp, turned it over and looked at the back, studied the photograph again, then handed it back.

Meanwhile Zakhov had been looking at the pictures on the walls. One of them was of a young man in uniform. He lit a cigarette, then took his card and put it back in his pocketbook.

'Your son?' he said, nodding at the photograph.

'Yes,' Grozdan said. 'He's in the Army, in Blagoevgrad.' At that moment, his wife came in again with a plate of radishes, honey, cheese and bread.

'Do you think we could have some anisette?' Zakhov said. 'I should like to drink the health of your son in the army.' She produced glasses and the bottle of anisette and they drank. The second glass seemed to thaw the old man. After a while his wife went out leaving them alone and Zakhov turned to him.

'I've come to you not just because you're President of the Co-operative Farm and all the rest of it, but also and largely because in Smolyan they told me that you were a loyal and responsible person in whom I could have absolute trust and confidence. You have, I know, been an active Party member since the beginning and those years of underground work will have taught you how to keep a secret. Now, I want to tell you why I have really come to Momchilovo, and to enlist your help. But I must make it clear that no one, not even your wife, must know anything about this. Ever.' He stared rather fixedly at the old man, who met his gaze unflinchingly. It was not easy to overawe—or impress—a member of these old peasant families. The old man nodded.

'Good,' Zakhov said. 'Now, this is where I need your help. First, I want to know the names of all who were absent from the village on the night of 22–3 August, which you will remember, I'm sure. Then I want to find out who in Momchilovo wears or has worn blue woollen gloves. If you find someone who does, or has, try also to discover when and where he bought them, or the wool, and also who, if anyone, knits for other people either in Momchilovo or the neighbouring villages.'

'Is that all?' Grozdan asked, a look of incredulity on his face. Counter-espionage and all the rest of it, and he wanted to know who had a pair of woollen gloves!

'For the moment, yes. It's more important than you might think.'

Then the old man leaned towards him and in a hoarse, confidential whisper, said, 'Are they going to hang him?'

'Who?'

'The schoolmaster.'

'That's not my business,' Zakhov said with a shrug of his shoulders.

At that moment the sun came out and a shaft of sunlight stabbed into the room through the little, curtained window. A bluebottle took off and began buzzing round the honey like a circling aircraft.

'But I imagine that what you discover may have something to do with the outcome,' Zakhov continued. 'We shall meet at Ilcho's at midday, I take it? If you have news for me, ask for a glass of lemonade, then I'll come and see you during the afternoon. Do you think you can manage this?'

The old man nodded and stroked his moustaches into place, one side with one hand, the other with the other hand. A vague smile hovered round his lips.

Zakhov got up and said goodbye to the old man's wife, kissing her hand in the most gallant old-fashioned way which made her shoot a glance of triumph at her rustic old husband, who had never done such a thing to her in all the years of their long married life; but he was busy trying to swat the fly and pretended that he had not noticed.

Zakhov next went to Iliazov's house. Georgi was on duty and so zealous that he refused to let him in, until the Major shouted at him. The ground-floor consisted of three rooms arranged round a big hall. This latter was a great sombre room, more like a medieval dungeon than the hall of a relatively modern house, and Zakhov felt that it only wanted a few chains hanging on the wall, a brazier and a rack to complete the scene. Three heavy, nail-studded oaken doors led from it; that on the left into a room that the Survey used as a store and where they also kept their instruments and maps. This was the room that had been broken into on the night of 23 August. The bar across the window had since been replaced with an even stouter one and the glass repaired. It was now also protected by shutters fastened with a bar and padlock.

Major Injov's reception of his visitor was scarcely cordial. He could think of nothing more irritating to have happened than to have an archaeologist poking about in the territory where he was engaged in such top secret work. Why had the Academy of Sciences been allowed to inflict this dreary-looking individual on him? He decided he would send a signal and ask for the fellow to be withdrawn.

The face that Zakhov studied as the Major read his letter of introduction from the Academy was pale and drawn. A bottle of tablets of bicarbonate of soda told its own tale. Also there was a mark on each shoulder strap as though at one time he had worn an extra pip there. Had the man been demoted? Was bitterness the reason for the coldness of his reception?

Finishing reading, the Major looked up and handed the letter back. There was a pause, then he said curtly, 'What is it you want of me?'

'Nothing particular,' Zakhov said. 'I just wanted to introduce myself, seeing that I shall be working in your area.'

'Well, now you have,' the Major said and looked down at some papers lying in front of him.

'Our jobs have certain points in common, though, don't you think?' Zakhov said.

'No, I don't.'

'Oh, why?' Zakhov pretended to be astonished. 'You go out into the mountains, studying the terrain; so must I.'

'Purely a superficial coincidence.'

Zakhov smiled. 'But a coincidence none the less, isn't it?'

The other did not reply.

'I want to define, relatively of course, the northern limits of the Momchilovo region, and I propose to explore the area to the south and south-east of the Karabair massif in search of traces of certain things that may be there.'

'Search then, by all means.'

'But you have been working in that same area; perhaps you could give me indications . . .'

'We have seen nothing that could be of interest to you.'

'That in itself is something!' Zakhov said. 'The fact that three specialists, trained observers like yourselves, have noticed nothing, is first-class negative evidence. What can I hope to see, especially on my own?'

'Go and find out.'

'I suppose, though, there is little point in my going where you have already been. You must of course have the co-ordinates of the area you have already surveyed?'

'Of course.' The Major took a cigarette from a box on the table and tapped it irritably before he lit it.

'Can I have them? That'll save me a lot of work.'

'No.'

'Why on earth not?'

'Because it will be good for you to do your own work. Also, what I do is for my department, which is quite different to yours. And why should I do extra work to encourage your laziness?'

'All right, all right,' Zakhov said. 'I only asked.'

'And I replied,' the Major said, and stood up.

Georgi was summoned to conduct Zakhov to the entrance. As they passed the door of the store-room, Zakhov dropped a watch-chain he was twiddling round his fingers and had to stop to pick it up; as he straightened up again he glanced at the lock. It was stout, but very old-fashioned and easy to pick.

It was a pity about the co-ordinates, because the frontier guards who had supplied the reference of the clandestine transmitter had not been able to say whether the Survey, which had been in the field at the time of the transmission, had been in that area then or not. The Major could have told him, but had not. However, the information would be there on the Survey's maps and to pick that lock would be child's play to Zakhov.

Now there was the new factor of the stone and the reason for its substitution. That surely must be connected?

Zakhov set off at a slow pace down the road to Lakité pondering these new factors: the stone, the Major's refusal to cooperate. It was a flat road, so thickly carpeted with grey dust that walking along it gave you the feeling of treading on carpet. Away back from the road were the rounded, hunchbacked shapes of the first hills, each carrying its bristling load of trees and bushes—mostly firs with an occasional myrtle or hawthorn. A hare came lolloping along and paused in the middle of the road scarcely fifty yards ahead of him, where it sat for a moment, long ears raised, then lolloped on again to the wood, the fringe of which it followed for a while before diving into a narrow opening between some bushes.

On the other side was a broad band of pastureland that ran all the way from Momchilovo to Lakité. It was covered with hundreds of white dots—sheep, from which came the occasional tinkle of a bell, an idyllically pastoral sound that those hills must have heard, year in, year out, for two, three—how many thousand years? In the distance a shepherd's dog barked—at him? Or at whom?

Then suddenly he thought of something that made him wheel round and stride back along the way he had come. On the outskirts of the village he asked a small girl with a very dirty face, who appeared to be in charge of a gaggle of suddenly vociferous geese, the way to the vet's house. A boy of that age might have been struck dumb by being addressed by a stranger, but not a girl. She gave him clear, explicit directions.

15

THE YOUNG VET had been up early, driven out of bed by his bête-noir, the cock. At four o'clock it had flown up onto the sill of his bedroom window, crowed and flapped its wings. For a moment he had wondered if it would be discouraged if he kept the window open and threw things at it when it flew up, but he decided that it was a malicious bird and that the only way to silence it was to wring its neck. Having been roused in this irritating way, he got up, dressed and went up to the farm to watch the early milking. He was a great stickler for hygiene and found two udder cloths that he considered anything but clean. And one of them was what the girl had been intending to use on Rashka, his record-breaking cow. He gave her a piece of his mind and received a nasty look in return. Then he went back to his room and began writing up his weekly report. He was busy on this when Avakum Zakhov came in smiling, laughing, apparently in excellent spirits. The vet was annoyed at being disturbed, but could scarcely turn his visitor out or tell him to come to the dispensary during consulting hours. Zakhov sat down without invitation, lounged back indolently in his chair and lit a cigarette. The way he behaved, you would have thought the two had been bosom cronies for years, instead of not having set eyes on each other before the previous day.

Zakhov came straight to the point:

'Doctor,' he said, 'do you know Anna Balabanova?'

The vet gaped at the unexpected question and nodded.

'A very interesting woman,' Zakhov went on.

'So you've discovered that already,' the vet said.

'What interests me is perhaps not what interests others,' said Zakhov, and leaning forward he showed the vet the card identifying him as a counter-espionage officer. The vet could not help wondering whether an extrovert like Zakhov could be a good counter-espionage man, but that was not his business. Zakhov blew out a cloud of smoke and the vet coughed. He detested smoke in his room.

'Anyway, I need some information about her, in particular what people say and think about her—you, for example, and others.'

'I'm afraid she doesn't come within the sphere of my vital interests,' the vet said. 'I only know what everyone else knows: that she's a good-looking woman, mature, a very good, hard worker who is likely to become the sheep expert of the Farm. Professionally, I have had occasion to compliment her on the cleanliness in her department there. She herself is always neat and trim—very wholesome, if I can use that expression: impeccably white blouse; clean, well-tended hands; clean scarf round her head. It's what I like to see.'

'Has she any lovers?' Zakhov asked.

'How should I know?' the vet said. 'I'm not one, at any rate, and I don't know of anyone who is. But it's nothing to do with me, so why should I? And gossip doesn't interest me.'

'Nor me. But facts do. And I want to find out if she has a visitor who comes to see her at night and uses the back way across the fence. If I go round asking questions, it will attract too much attention, but someone from here could do so quite naturally and no one would think anything of it. Will you help? This is important, you know. It's not just a question of gossip.'

No young man could help feeling slightly flattered at being asked to help in counter-espionage, even if the task was nothing more exciting than this. In a way the young man felt glad that no more was required of him. Then Zakhov went on to explain that a man's life, as well as more general questions of national security, depended on the result of his investigations, and naturally the vet agreed to do whatever he could. Zakhov's face lit up when he heard this, as though something really big had happened. He was almost over-acting.

After a little more talk he got up to go. Reminding the young vet of what he wanted, he suggested that Anna Balabanova's neighbours would be the right people to supply the information, especially the female members of the households, but that he mustn't appear too eager or sinister. If he had any news for him, he said, he could find him that evening at Ilcho's and they could leave together and talk as they walked along.

Now, as it happened, Dr Nacheva, who interested the young vet far more than Anna Balabanova, lodged in one of the neighbouring houses when she was in Momchilovo and so would probably know all there was to be known. And, being very human, she would no doubt be only too willing to tell anything she knew to the discredit of one whom she must regard as a potential rival; so he decided to go and see if she was at home and, if so, see what he could elicit from her.

His heart beat faster than usual as he entered the courtyard of the house in which the doctor lodged. It was, in fact, the first time he had been there. In the yard there was only the owner of the house, grinding pepper.

'Good day, good day,' he said. 'How are you? What news of your husband?'—he was working in Madan—'and yourself?'

She had a pretty, narrow face with a very white complexion, which a lot of people found attractive.

'My husband is very well,' she said. 'And earning well, too.'

'And the pig?' the vet said, suddenly remembering that it was one of his patients. 'Has he got his appetite back?'

'Appetite! He's eating me out of house and home, but somehow he doesn't seem to be putting on enough weight. I'm not too happy about him.' She sighed and, putting down the pepper mill, got up off her stool.

She had chubby cheeks like a cupid.

'Come and see him,' she said. 'Perhaps you can prescribe something.'

They went to the back of the house where the pig-sty was. The pig was lying on its side in the sun and grunted a greeting as they appeared. It was enormous, like a giant cornucopia with tiny eyes and feet. The vet looked at it for a while, then said, 'I should hardly call him thin. In fact, I should have said that he was doing quite all right. Plenty of food there for Christmas.'

For a while they stood side by side, leaning on the wall of the sty, regarding the pig.

'You're not really worried, are you?' he said.

'No-o,' she said and there was a mischievous twinkle in her eye. 'Not really.' She sighed.

'Is the doctor at home?' the vet asked in a tone of voice he hoped sounded casual.

'No. She's at Lakité. Won't be here at all today.'

Silence.

'And how's Anna Balabanova's pig?' he said.

She threw back her head and laughed.

'Her pig?' she exclaimed. 'What makes you think she's got a pig? What on earth would she need one for?'

'Oh,' he said, 'she might get married.'

'She!' Mrs Nadka exclaimed and a steely glint came into her

eye. 'Why should she bother, when she already has someone who comes to her at night, by the back way, too, across the fence!'

'Across the fence? You can't mean it!'

'Do you think I'm inventing it?' she said indignantly. 'Before the schoolmaster began courting the game-warden's widow, she behaved fairly well, because she had hopes of him. But now . . !'

'Now?' he queried.

She came so close he could feel her breath on him.

'She's not one to go for small fry,' she said.

'You must be imagining things,' he said.

'I haven't that sort of imagination,' she said, her voice rising slightly with indignation. 'Anyway, with my own eyes I've seen that Icherenski going to her house at night.'

The young man could have kissed her. This indeed was something to report. His eyes danced with elation. The woman's gaze became wondering, then her expression softened and there was a light in her eye that made him feel that he had better beat a hasty retreat, if he did not want to become involved.

'Your pig's all right,' he said turning away. 'If anything, I should say you gave him too much to eat.'

With that he went, leaving her rather puzzled and perhaps disappointed.

The other regulars were already at table when the vet reached the tavern. Krumov had made a special effort and there was roast chicken, puff cheese pastry and the inevitable pickled pimentos. With all this went a dry white wine that smelled of sun-warmed amber.

Zakhov and Icherenski were clinking glasses as the young vet came in, and he heard Icherenski say, 'I trust your first night in Momchilovo was a good one. You slept undisturbed, I hope.'

'Thank you,' Zakhov said, taking another sip of wine. 'I had an excellent night. With a little amusement thrown in: someone almost came into my room. I wanted to see him so as to put him right as to the geography of the place, but he skipped off too quickly for me.'

Icherenski and the captain laughed.

'You ought to have gone after him. But I can assure you, he will not have meant any harm. Some jealous suitor come to satisfy himself that his beloved was not having a late tête-à-tête with the new lodger. There are Othellos everywhere, even in Momchilovo. You should be used to it.'

'I? I never give cause for that. I'm a virtuous chap. Don't I look it?'

And so they went on jestingly, the remarks getting more and more pointed until old Grozdan intervened.

'Comrades,' he said, 'you're really going too far. I don't like it. Anna Balabanova may have no children, and she is a widow, but she's an honest, decent woman. She does her work well and we all think highly of her. There are absolutely no grounds for the hints you're making.'

'Love,' said Icherenski, 'is everywhere and means different things to different people. To some it's just how-do-you-do and goodbye. To others it is a hieroglyphic that they do not even try to interpret. To others again it is a cause of sighs and insomnia—in their own beds, of course! To those like old Grozdan it means a house and children and a faithful wife: a good healthy concept of great use to society. To one and all it is a mixed blessing, a source of joy and care, of great pleasure and some anxiety.

'You all know that every Saturday I mount my motorcycle and ride to Plovdiv, but don't imagine there's any romantic charm about those trips! I arrive in the late afternoon or evening. I get myself a room in an hotel and ring up my wife. She, poor woman, lives with her aunt where she has to sleep in the same room as the children, so you will understand why I cannot go there. Thus we have only a few hours to ourselves each week, and for that I ride eighty miles. But I'm not complaining.

'I sometimes wonder whether I should have been happier if I had chosen a sedentary occupation where I should have been always in the one place and with my wife all the time. I rather doubt it. That sort of life is rather like a house without a fireplace. You must have a certain amount of anxiety and a few cares in order to be really happy.'

He fell silent, picked up his glass and took another sip of wine.

'Talking of love,' he said, looking round at us with a gentle smile, 'let me tell you a little story in this connection which concerns our unfortunate schoolmaster. He may perhaps be hanged, as our archaeologist here seems to think; if so, no doubt he will have deserved it, but let us also remember the good that was in him.

'Grozdan here can tell you better than I the benefits he has brought Momchilovo: how he has taught apiculture and shown people how to grow fruit and prune their trees, and also, I believe, a way of increasing the fat content of their cheese.' He looked across at the old man, who nodded. 'I want to tell you about another side of him. First, I must explain that Metodi regarded me as a friend because I gave him help and assistance on various things he was doing in the sphere of crystallography. He wanted to make a complete collection of crystals and stones for the school, but he was not experienced enough and asked me if I would help, which I did to the best of my ability. From the academic point of view, of course, he was just an amateur and to some extent a crank, yet there was at times something sublime about his enthusiasm and his belief that he would make discoveries of real importance. You couldn't help liking him for it and admiring his keenness and the work he was prepared to put into things, at the same time as feeling sorry for him, when he was obviously set on making a fool of himself. Anyway, he regarded me as his friend and used to confide in me some of his little secrets, especially after a glass or two of wine.

'What I am about to tell you is, as you will see, directly concerned with what we have just been discussing: love.

'Three years ago a new forest-warden came to Momchilovo. He was a keen hunter, and he and Metodi struck up an immediate friendship. People thought that the bond was their mutual love of shooting and the mountains, but that was only half the truth. The other half concerns the flowering of a late love. I mean between the wife of the game warden and the schoolmaster.

'The former was ten years younger than her husband. They had a little girl, but she was living with her grandmother because the warden's cottage was miles away from anywhere and the man did not intend to remain in Momchilovo for longer than he had to and was hoping to return soon to what he called civilization. His wife was a slight, fair-haired woman, kind and gentle, the very opposite of the schoolmaster and thus the exact sort of person to awaken his love. It was a genuine but very innocent love, limited to looks and the clasp of their hands as they said good-morning and goodbye.

'So, to her great regret, Anna Balabanova saw her lodger going more and more frequently to the game-warden's house, and more and more often the game he shot was eaten there in return for the coffee and other delicacies with which he was entertained.

'One winter's day the two men decided to see if they could not shoot some of the Zmeitza wolves that were beginning to raid the near-by farmsteads. They set out together, but the schoolmaster soon realized that he had left his woollen muffler in the game-warden's house and went back to get it. He was gone such a short time that he cannot have been more than a minute or two inside; what transpired there, what was done or said, I do not know, but whatever it was the schoolmaster was distrait and uncommunicative when he rejoined the other. He walked along with his eyes on the ground—thinking of what? Certainly not of wolves. That is how, when the mist came down suddenly, as it can do in these parts, the two men were separated as effectively as if they had been a hundred miles apart. You know the rest of the story. The wolves took advantage of the mist to steal up on the warden and they had him down before he could fire a shot. It was only their snarling that told the schoolmaster what was happening and by the time he arrived on the scene, the warden was dead and a good deal of him eaten.

'What happened then? The schoolmaster limited his personal expenses to the absolute minimum, living pretty well on bread and water, and with what he saved by doing this he bought the game-warden's widow a knitting machine. She had by then got her young daughter home to live with her and the girl was attending school in Momchilovo. Every month Metodi put a third of his salary into an account he had opened in the girl's name in the post-office savings bank.

'That is love for you, indeed; sparked off, one supposes, by what transpired during that brief minute or two, but scarcely more, they had alone together when Metodi went back for his muffler.

'One would think that, after an interval, this love would have blossomed out into a reciprocal love; yet that does not appear to have happened and it is that which prompted my question: what is love?

'When they meet, whether outdoors in the sun or indoors in the kitchen, the girl, the widow's daughter, will always be there or somewhere close at hand. That he can be content with such a love tells one a lot about the schoolmaster. Not, unfortunately, whether he is guilty of the crimes of which he is now accused; let's hope that he is not and that we shall see him sitting here among us again.'

There was a long silence when Icherenski finished and for the rest of the meal there was little more than desultory conversation. They left in a body. Zakhov appeared greatly interested in the two motorcycles—Icherenski and Christoforov each had one—and touched them here and there. Then he and the young vet walked off together.

'Well,' he said, 'did you discover anything?'

The vet hesitated, then told Zakhov what Mrs Nadka had said, expecting him to be surprised or delighted, but he was neither the one nor the other. He just yawned and thanked him in a tone of utter indifference and boredom.

16

AVAKUM ZAKHOV strolled on through the brilliant sunlight, digesting the information the young vet had given him. At its face value it could mean a lot and give a different turn to his investigations; but Mrs Nadka could very easily be jumping to conclusions that were not justified. The visitor she had seen might have been going to the junk-room as had the clandestine visitor of the previous night.

Looking up, he saw old Grozdan standing near the house, evidently waiting for him.

'Did you forget the signal we agreed?' Zakhov said jocularly.

'No,' the old man replied, his face unsmiling, 'but there wasn't any lemonade.'

Then he told Zakhov how he had been to the Co-operative

where they had told him that they never kept knitting wool of any kind. Both he and the local secretary of the Party had racked their brains trying to remember who had worn blue gloves that winter and they had come to the conclusion that no one in Momchilovo or the surrounding villages could have worn blue gloves, at least not regularly, otherwise they would have remembered.

'So that did not get us very far,' the old man said. 'Ruddy waste of time, in fact,' he added. 'As to the other matter, those who were absent from the village on the night that interests you; we know this: Anna Balabanova spent that night up at the farm. Her team was on duty then and she was there from six in the evening until dawn. Old Manassi—Kuzman Christoforov has a room in his house—had gone off the day before to see to his beehives up in the mountains. Icherenski, as you know, goes to Plovdiv every Saturday and so was not here. And that evening Captain Kaludiev was at a party given by the women workers of Lakité. So far, that's all I have been able to find out.'

Zakhov appeared quite unimpressed. With a quick glance round him, he pulled a cloth from a pocket of his raincoat that he carried over his arm and, bending down, wiped the dust off his shoes. As he did so, Mrs Nadka appeared in her yard and began calling her hens. There was a confused cackling and a concerted fluttering, leaping rush as she began strewing grain and household scraps and a moment later she was surrounded by gobbling birds.

Zakhov straightened up and looked at the old man.

'Thank you for your help,' he said. 'You may not see how, but it will come in useful.'

Then he opened the outer door and went in.

Going up to his room, he lay down on the bed, that being the only place there where he was comfortable. From where he lay he could see through the open window as far as the person who had climbed the old pine tree outside the window. No wollen gloves were sold locally, nor even the wherewithal to knit them, because the Co-operative issued a considerable quantity of unspun wool to each household, the female members of which spun it and knitted up the yarn as they liked; thus the blue gloves must have been obtained elsewhere, as would be the case if the 'criminal' was not a local resident, or specially knitted, if he was.

The latter could scarcely be the case as the filaments obtained from the bar and the bark were long and spiral, whereas the filaments of homespun are short and usually straight. The wool from which the gloves were made was of machine manufacture and this was seldom, if ever, to be found on sale in rural areas. You could, of course, buy ready-made gloves in stores in the cities and bigger towns, but these were almost always light or dark brown, or grey. He could not remember having seen ones of any other colour, certainly none that were blue. Thus if the gloves were specially knitted, who had knitted them? Was there anyone at Momchilovo who could have done it? Of course! The warden's widow, the wife of the man the wolves had eaten, the fringe of the Zmeitza, which was shrouded in mist. Heavy clouds came up and blotted out the sun; then the wind got up and a scurry of rain struck the roof. Somewhere a door banged.

Trying to review the situation and fit the day's new facts into the picture, he decided that so far he had made little or no progress. If only they could decode those messages! Why had the previous night's visitor swapped the stone? And who was he? Had he got all that he wanted, or would he return? What would his next step be? There were so many questions to which as yet he had no answers and the sheer weight of them closed his eyelids.

He woke with a start, feeling cold and shivery. He got up, lit a cigarette and began walking round the room to get his circulation going. Was Anna at home, he wondered. If so, there ought to be a fire in her big room. But she would expect him to talk or at least pay attention to her, and he must think. Perhaps the cold would help him. Where to start?

The person who broke into the room at Iliazov's, or who pretended to break in, had worn blue woollen gloves; so had the woman whom Parashkevov was now courting: he had given her a knitting machine. Where did she get the wool she knitted up? Had she ever had any that was blue?

But if someone was wanting a pair of gloves just to wear so as to avoid leaving fingerprints, why not wear leather gloves or even a pair of harvester's gloves? Why woollen ones, perhaps specially knitted for the occasion? Did these country people who were mostly employed in stock-breeding wear harvester's gloves and if so could you buy them locally? If not, then it would seem that one could arrive at two conclusions: (a), the person who wore the gloves had received an unexpected commission which necessitated wearing gloves; and (b), he had not possessed a pair of gloves and had not been in a position to go to a town where gloves could be bought before having to carry out this commission.

Now this person could have been the accused, Metodi Parashkevov, but if it was not, which he, Zakhov, was convinced was the case, then it could only be one of the team of geologists. Zakhov decided that he could do without them in the village for a day or two.

He ran out of the room and downstairs to see if Anna Balabanova was back from the farm yet. No, there was nobody about, not a soul to be seen anywhere. Locking the door of his room, he undid the fastenings of his hold-all and produced the portable transmitter he had collected at Smolyan. He had the aerial erected in no time at all and while he tapped out the call sign, he quickly coded a brief message: *Require all members of the Geological Survey absent from village for at least twenty-*

four hours. Also everything about Boyan Icherenski before joining Survey. Sofia answered, the message was given and acknowledged, the aerial dismantled and the set stowed away in the hold-all again.

Dusk was falling. The approach of evening had brought a fine drizzle that made the last of the day damp and cold. He felt a great longing for the warmth of a fire and, giving way to a sudden impulse, he went to the woodshed beside the disused stable, picked up the axe and began chopping firewood. The need to watch his stroke drove all other thoughts from his mind: blue wool, gloves, geologists, he thought of nothing but getting his wood into the right length and size. The pile beside him had assumed quite satisfactory proportions, and he was thinking that he must stop because there was not light enough to see by, when he sensed that there was someone standing behind him. He knew that it was Anna Balabanova but pretended not to be aware of her.

Then he heard her say:

'But how nice of you! I never expected to get this help.'

Zakhov drove the axe into the chopping-block, straightened up and turned towards her. Her headscarf was wet and drops of moisture glistened on a few black wisps that had escaped from it. He took a step towards her and was aware of the fresh, heady smell of her body.

'I thought it would be nice to have a really big fire this evening,' he said. 'So that you could be warm and rest by it after a day's work. And, perhaps, I might join you.'

She was looking up at him. There was no mocking now in either her eyes or her voice as she said, 'That was a nice thought, but I'm not tired—or cold.' Then, with a mischievous glint in her eyes, 'But it's a good idea even so.' With a swift, graceful movement she bent down and began filling her apron with logs.

As he stood looking down at her, he felt his throat contract with an emotion he had not felt for a long time. The skin on the back of her neck, where the hair fell away from the nape—he bent down as though to kiss it, but stopped himself in time—or should he have gone on and done it?

He picked up some logs.

Together they walked back to the house and deposited the logs beside the hearth. In a minute or two she had blown up the embers beneath the white ash and was sitting back on her heels, her face flushed and smiling, while the busy flames licked round the logs and sent huge black shadows dancing round the room. She took off her scarf and shook out her hair, and he decided that the best place for his hands was in his pockets, so he kept them there stubbornly. He wanted her, wanted to make love to her, yet something was holding him back. What? The schoolmaster was courting the game-warden's widow, not her; there was no one whom he would harm, if he did make love to her. Was it just because he was on duty and must not compromise himself? She would not care whether he was an archaeologist or counter-espionage officer. He was a man and his body called to hers—he was sure of that—and that was all that mattered to either of them. So why not?

Then she got to her feet, saying, 'Now, let's see what there is to eat.'

She walked off into the shadows at the end of the long room and into the larder. Returning, she announced, 'Eggs, ham, cheese and rather stale bread. Will you stay?'

'No chef in Sofia could tempt me away,' he said, and he knew that he meant it.

After they had eaten and the table had been cleared, she came and sat on a low stool beside him. As he smoked his pipe, he gazed at her quite openly. Her blouse was loosely cut and fell provocatively open as she leaned slightly forward, hands clasped round her knees, staring into the fire, busy with her own thoughts. She had pulled her skirt up towards her knees and her calves shone like copper in the firelight.

'Would you do something for me?' he said.

'That depends.'

'A favour.'

'What is it?'

'In return for my chopping your wood.'

'Does that merit a big reward?'

'None at all really—but I would love you to do something for me.'

'What?' She looked up at him softly.

'Sing for me. One of the old songs.'

'Just one?' She laughed softly. 'I have not much of a voice, you know. But if you like—I will. Tonight you are the master of the house.'

She rocked back on the stool, hands clasped round her knees, just her toes on the ground and his pulses raced as his eyes followed the line of her neck deep down. Then in a rather husky voice she began to sing.

It was an age-old song, a song that Orpheus might have sung—or were the days when he lived happier ones, in which people were never lovelorn? (Anyway, someone who could sing like Orpheus probably had a fan club of teenage Thracian girls offering themselves at every step he took.) In the song she sang, a young man inquires of his beloved if she is really an ordinary mortal and not a goddess from the heavens or a wood-nymph, as he fears she may be. To him she seems too lovely to be entirely human. But the girl, annoyed to find herself set on a pedestal and worshipped when she wants to be taken in a pair of strong arms and made love to, replies that she is mortal indeed, born of her mother and nourished with her milk like any child, so that her skin is like milk and her eyes the colour of the grapes from which came the wine that she offers him.

Anna sang at first with her eyes downcast, fixed on the glowing logs, but then she turned and looked up into his face: lovely she was indeed, and incontestably human.

He puffed at his pipe furiously, trying hard to pretend to himself that the pounding of his heart was not choking him.

She stopped and leaned forward to stir up the fire. As she did so her blouse fell forward and involuntarily he stretched out his arms, but she was no longer looking at him and appeared not to notice.

'Thank you.' he said. 'That was so lovely. I believe you must be the local wood nymph.'

'Gracious, no! Wood nymphs are always young and lovely. At least, they are in this part of the world.'

'That's exactly what I meant,' he said.

'Nymph or no, I think I should like a glass of wine,' she said, and, getting up, went to the back of the room. He turned as she came back and the flickering flames showed him that the door to the other room now stood open. She put the bottle and two glasses on the floor beside him and pulled her stool a little closer. Now, she had only to lean back an inch or two and she could rest her shoulder against his legs.

They drank, and for a while neither spoke. Then, as his hand was on its way back from putting down his glass, it touched her shoulders. The slightest pressure of his fingers overcame the two-inch gap. Then she leaned her head back and turning her face so that she could look into his, she sang another song, one that Eurydice might have sung.

There was a click from the latch as the door shut, after which the bulging sides of the two copper pans that hung on the wall reflected the hearth in which the leaping flames grew lower and lower. An empty chair, an empty stool and two half-empty glasses.

17

THE MORNING was misty and there was a chill in the air. Zakhov put on his raincoat and, locking the door behind him, set off for the tavern. Anna must have been up at the farm already. Zakhov hummed the air of the song she had sung him the night before and smiled.

Marco Krumov brought him his breakfast: two boiled eggs and some cheese. When he had finished, Zakhov put his hand in his pocket for his purse, but the taverner, noticing it, stopped him.

'Look,' he said, 'why bother yourself settling up after every meal and so making life more complicated for me? Why not do as the others do: they give me a hundred-leva note on the first of each month and I give them a card on which they record everything they have. Then, at the end of the month, I tot it all up and give them back anything they haven't spent, or, if they have spent more, they make up the difference. Wouldn't that be more convenient?'

'As you wish,' Zakhov said and produced a hundred-leva note, in exchange for which he received a card of very ordinary board ruled like graph paper. Krumov showed him a number of others he had. Zakhov was intrigued to see that Captain Kaludiev's writing was in illegible scribble worthy of a busy doctor, while Kuzman Christoforov's was large and beautifully formed, almost copper-plate. Icherenski's was an obviously energetic hand, perfectly legible but tiny. And yet people say you tell a person's character by his handwriting, Zakhov thought, as he handed the cards back to Krumov, who flung them all into a drawer in his desk. Then he asked the way to the house where Marie, the game-warden's widow, lived and was told that it was on the same side of the village as the Survey's H.Q., but a short way beyond it across a stretch of waste ground all humps and holes, overgrown with bushes and thistles. There were two or three tortuous paths through this waste, one of which went past Marie's house and on to join the road to Lakité.

It was a low, single-storeyed house, like almost all the others in the village, built of brick, on three sides of a square, with a slate roof and a newly whitewashed front. This latter and the obvious cleanness of the curtains at the windows gave it an air of meticulous, trim neatness that spoke of loving care. In the middle of its little yard was a shaggy pear tree, its aged trunk imprisoned in the clasp of a seat that invited you to rest beneath its branches and enjoy the gaiety of the bed of dahlias and geraniums that followed the line of the house.

Zakhov knocked and waited, knocked again, and again. No answer. Going back to the track, he saw that his arrival had drawn an old crone out of the next-door house and she was now spreading or pretending to spread something on her fence, while her beady old eyes suspiciously watched everything he did. When he spoke to her, she just glared at him, but finally told him that Marie and the girl had gone off to the farm to fetch their milk and would not be back for another half-hour.

Zakhov set off back the way he had come, but then leaving the path he climbed a short but steep mound, on the other side of which he found the wall at the back of Iliazov's house. This, he realized, must have been where Metodi Parashkevov had jumped down when taking the short cut through the courtyard on that fateful night. For a moment or two he stood taking in the scene, but then his attention was diverted by the sound of voices calling and an unusual air of bustle about the

Survey and, hurrying down the mound, he entered the courtyard by the main gate.

Two mules were standing under the great elm tree patiently letting themselves be laden with a variety of bundles, cases and surveyor's instruments. The soldier, Georgi, and a mule-driver were lashing the loads under the supervision of Icherenski and Kaludiev; while Kuzman Christoforov stood a little to one side, a cigarette between his lips, gazing up into the sky as though planning to survey that.

'Hallo, where are you all off to?' Zakhov exclaimed, pretending to be surprised. 'You look as if you were going to be away for some time,' he added sadly, eyeing the mules' heavy loads.

'I admire your perspicacity,' Kaludiev said, thrusting his cap onto the back of his head. Icherenski did not even look round. He seemed unaware that the archaeologist was there.

'Yes, we're off, my dear fellow,' the Captain said flinging his arm out in a wide gesture. 'Duty calls us to fresh exploits in the cause of peace.'

'Fine lot we'll get done,' Icherenski said looking up from the bag in which he had been rummaging, 'if you even forget to pack a theodolite.'

Kaludiev swore and ran off to fetch one, while Icherenski turned and looked at Zakhov, but said nothing: he did not even greet him.

'Going far?' Zakhov asked.

'You shouldn't ask questions,' Icherenski replied. 'What we do is no concern of yours, nor has it anything to do with the work you have been sent here to do.'

'Oh, come now,' Zakhov said, smiling. 'I should have thought that the opposite was the case. You can scarcely help going to places that will be of particular interest to me too.'

'Where we go is our affair,' Icherenski went on, frowning. 'Don't meddle with things that don't concern you. It's a bad habit of yours. If you go on sticking your nose into everything, one day you'll find yourself without one.'

'God forbid,' Zakhov exclaimed, putting his hand to his nose. 'I'm very fond of my nose. I have the highest opinion of it. It's a very good one—it's won all sorts of prizes.'

'Buzz off,' Icherenski said and the tone—if not the expression—was that of a soldier giving an order, very different from the gay insouciance of Icherenski the tavern companion.

Zakhov put up his hand in salutation, nodded to Christoforov, turned and walked away. As he passed the soldier, Georgi, he asked him if he was going to act as escort.

'What, me? Not likely, Comrade,' Georgi exclaimed. 'There would be nobody to guard the H.Q., if I did.'

'You're fortunate,' Zakhov said, looking up at the leaden clouds from which a slight drizzle had begun to fall. 'You'll be much snugger where you are. This isn't the weather for trekking.'

Then Zakhov walked off down the road in the direction of Lakité. As soon as he was round the next bend and out of sight of Iliazov's house, he left the road and scrambled up the side of a hillock and finding himself a dry sheltered place among some bushes, from where he had a good view of the road, settled himself there as comfortably as circumstances permitted, lit a pipe and prepared to wait.

At the end of about an hour, by which time the rain was just beginning to start on the long journey down his neck, Zakhov saw the geologists' cavalcade appear on the road. In front came the Major, followed by Icherenski and Kaludiev walking together; behind them came the two mules, and the rear was brought up by the muleteer and Christoforov. He watched the group until it had disappeared round the next bend, where it was hidden from view by the shoulder of a hill, then, knocking out his pipe, he got to his feet and walked off westwards at as brisk a pace as the bushes and the roughness of the ground allowed. In about ten minutes he came out onto a broad path which he calculated must lead to Marie's house. He had only followed it for a few minutes, when he saw the house in front of him.

Marie was a slight, rather frail-looking woman with blue eyes, fair hair, sloping shoulders and a sad, faintly worried expression. You could imagine her being bullied, even beaten by the wrong sort of husband, but also see that in decent men she would arouse all the chivalry that is latent in them, even in the twentieth century. She came to the outer door in answer to Zakhov's summons on the knocker, and stood there without inviting him in, while he explained his errand. There was a surprisingly warm, vibrant quality about her voice that made you aware that here was a person in whom there might well be hidden depths. She kept glancing across at her neighbour's house as though she knew that the old harpy there would be watching all that went on. Noticing this, Zakhov said, 'Your neighbour seems very interested in your——' he was about to say 'clients', but thinking better of it, changed it to 'business'.

She did not reply.

'I understand that you knit wonderful gloves,' Zakhov went on. 'My work necessitates my being out of doors most of the time, and I've come to ask you if you could knit me a nice pair of gloves rather quickly.'

'I could indeed,' the woman replied, 'but I'm afraid you will have to supply the wool.'

'But why? Haven't you any?'

Marie shook her head.

'None at all?'

Another shake of her head.

'What a pity,' Zakhov said and began lighting his pipe. 'I was shown a pair of blue gloves you had knitted and liked them enormously and felt that I would like a pair just like them.'

'I have no wool of that colour now,' she said.

'You've used it all?' Zakhov exclaimed. 'You had some quite recently.'

A frown of puzzlement appeared on the woman's forehead. She was staring down at her hands. 'Oh no, it's much longer ago than that,' she said. 'I had a small amount of blue wool in the spring or very early summer; but it was very little and I was keeping it for myself.'

'Which you ought to have done,' Zakhov said. 'You have blue eyes and that wool would have gone very well with them. You should have stuck on to it and told . . .' He paused and tapped his head with a gesture of impatience. 'Now, I've gone and forgotten the man's name.'

'Kuzman Christoforov,' she put in helpfully.

Zakhov nodded and puffed at his pipe a few times in silence, then he went on:

'That's it, Kuzman. He was fortunate. But why didn't you make his gloves of a different wool?'

'Because I didn't have any and he didn't want to have to buy more.'

'And now you've none at all?'

'No,' she said and her voice was very quiet. She shivered.

'I'm sorry,' Zakhov said, 'and for you,' he added and her cheeks flamed.

Then, nodding his head in the direction of the circular seat under the old pear tree that he could see across her shoulder, he said, 'That, I take it, is where you and our friend, the poor schoolmaster, sat and talked on the night of 22 August?'

She looked dumbfounded, then frightened.

'Don't be afraid,' he said gently. 'I am his friend and he has taken me into his confidence.'

Then he took hurried leave of her and walked away. But his heart was so full of pity for her, incorrigible romantic that he was, that after a few steps he wheeled round and went striding back to the open doorway in which Marie still stood, unable to comprehend what it was all about.

'I nearly forgot the most important thing of all,' he said, thrusting his hand into a pocket of his raincoat and bringing out a fountain pen with a gold nib and a case ornamented with a tiny ruby.

'The schoolmaster sent this for your daughter, for her to write her homework with.'

Marie's hand was trembling as she took the pen and she began blinking rapidly.

'You're not to worry about him,' Zakhov said. 'This beastly business will turn out all right. He'll be back in the village, perhaps even before the first snow.'

She was biting her lip, struggling to keep her tears back and quite unable to speak.

As he walked away, Zakhov felt better. He had had no right to say what he had; in fact, if Colonel Manov knew about it he would have to give him the sack. One word from Marie and his cover would be burst and he himself completely compromised; but somehow he did not think that Marie would say a word, even to her daughter.

Manassi's house was on the western fringe of the village, near the road that led from Momchilovo to Smolyan and Plovdiv. Between the road and the house was a large expanse of grass, while the forest and the mountain itself had stolen right close up to the back of the house as though engaged on a monstrous game of grandmother's footsteps.

Manassi was a widower, had been one for many years and now that his only child, a son, had married and gone to work at Kurjali, he was all on his own. As a result he lived most of the time up at the Co-operative Farm, and only came to his cottage once a week or so to keep an eye on it and get anything he might need. It was a small cottage, low and very old. There were only two rooms. The old kitchen-living-room on the ground floor with a low raftered ceiling and trodden earthen floor and, upstairs, a bedroom with an enormous family bed capable of accommodating a married couple and innumerable small children. It was in this room that Kuzman, the engineer, now lodged. When old Manassi was on one of his infrequent visits he slept on a narrow sofa near the hearth.

A mist had now come down, so there was little risk indeed of anyone seeing him in that secluded spot, but even so Zakhov chose to approach the house from behind, out of the cover of the shadows of the trees. He did not even have to use his jemmy on the lock. All that was necessary was to use it to raise the door a little and then pull it towards him, and the lock slipped out of the rusty keeper.

Quietly he closed the door behind him and stood for a minute or two without moving in order to accustom his eyes to the sudden gloom. The place smelled of damp and resinous pine wood. It was almost bare of furniture: a narrow sofa covered with rustic rugs, probably home woven, stood against the inner wall close to the hearth with its little pile of cold ash; out towards the middle of the room was a rectangular cupboard that seemed to do duty as a table and which proved to contain the old man's few clothes. Along the other walls were a few shelves, their edges studded with hooks from which nothing hung, and on them stood an occasional worn earthenware plate or an abandoned blackened cooking-pot. The place scarcely looked lived in. On the far side, away from the hearth, was an open door from which a flight of wooden stairs led up to the floor above. Down these stairs came more light than was able to filter through the small panes of the one little window, for these were almost opaque with soot and flyblow.

Going upstairs, Zakhov paused on the threshold of the upstairs room. From what he had seen of Christoforov, he expected to find his room a dirty, disorderly shambles, yet to his amazement it was spick and span, the things all neatly arranged or put away. There was the meticulous exactness and tidiness of a barracks. The cover on the bed was smooth: not a fold or a wrinkle to be seen. There was a table that had probably come from the room downstairs, the enormous bed and a chest of drawers. There was no cupboard or wardrobe and the engineer's suits and coats hung from stout pegs deeply embedded in the thick old wall.

He felt quite sure that the incriminating blue gloves were not there, but that was not evidence admissible in a court of law and he had to make a thorough search. He began with the table, an ordinary table without drawers or any place for keeping things; instead there was a board of smooth planed wood with one or two nails stuck into it on which all sorts of papers were spiked. He removed and scrutinized these papers one by one: there were official movement orders, receipts for rent, pay slips—all in Kuzman's name except the rent receipts, and with illegible signatures and government stamps. The papers were in chronological order starting at the end of April that year. He got out his pocket torch and magnifying glass and examined each, but there was no sign of anything that could be a cryptogram, let alone a microdot. Having subjected each paper to this scrutiny he returned it to its nail in the order in which it had come off. Next he turned his attention to the bed: pillow, mattress, underneath. Nothing. Then he started on the man's clothes, systematically turning out pockets, examining hems, linings and all other possible hiding-places, but found only a few loose matches and some sunflower seeds, until from the breast pocket of a sports jacket he pulled a pair of sun-glasses. There was nothing in any way unusual about these, but closer examination revealed one thing which made him wonder. The lenses, especially the part near the frame, were covered with a fine white dust. Under the magnifying glass this proved to be composed of microscopic particles of stone.

Now, the roads round Momchilovo are all dirt roads and the dust on them is nothing but powdered earth, which, of course, readily adheres to the lenses of spectacles, especially when they are moist with sweat off the wearer's face. The finely powdered dust on the sun-glasses was, he knew, dust that you get off roads where the surface is macadam or paved. Now, when you walk along a road a certain amount of dust out of the air will adhere to your glasses, while if you are riding a motorcycle or driving in a car, the speed through the air will cause many more particles to adhere, especially in hot weather when there will be more moisture on the glass. Thus these sun-glasses told Zakhov that Christoforov had driven a motorcycle or a car along a macadam road in hot weather and presumably quite recently. Further investigation of the pocket produced a piece of thin paper folded into a narrow strip. Unfolding this Zakhov discovered that it was a receipt for petrol bought from an all-night filling station in Plovdiv. It was dated 22 August. Making a note of the number of the receipt and the name of the filling station, Zakhov folded it up again and put it back at the bottom of the pocket. Thus, making sure that everything was as he had found it, he left the room and the cottage, making sure that the lock clicked back into place as he closed the door behind him.

He went straight to the Co-operative Farm, which possessed the only telephone in the village, and from there rang up the authorities in Smolyan and asked for a jeep to be sent at once. So as to avoid its coming into the village, and also to gain time, he said that he would start walking up the road so that it would probably meet him a mile or so from Momchilovo.

He then set off through the drizzle which effectively laid the dust but failed to damp his spirits which were now high. In fact, he was almost jubilant.

He was well beyond the village, probably even out of earshot of the last of the houses, when the jeep arrived. It backed onto the verge, turned, he got in and it jolted off back the way it had come.

The sun came out as the jeep topped the last rise before the Smolyan valley and in an instant the shallow Smolyan lakes were transformed into millions of facets of sun-glitter, so dazzling that you no longer saw the necks and jutting arms of land between them. The first impact was almost blinding, but as they dropped downhill the angle changed and the scene became normal. Zakhov was too intent on his mission now to appreciate the natural beauties that surrounded him and remained unaware of the conical shapes of the few trees left each on its spit of land and of the autumnal colouring that had come over all but the evergreens. Behind them a deer belled, but he did not hear it.

Reaching the main square in Smolyan, the jeep turned down a side street and pulled up at a side door of the administrative building. Zakhov went inside. Ten minutes later he emerged and spoke to the driver, who got down. Zakhov took his place behind the wheel, started the engine, turned and drove off.

A sense of urgency, of which so far in this case he had not really been aware, had taken possession of him and he drove fast, so that it was still only the middle of the afternoon when he drove across the long bridge with its innumerable piers, turned left along the embankment beneath the long line of the poplars each now casting a long shadow onto the water, and then right again to the divisional police station, where a plainclothes man was waiting for him on instructions from Smolyan. The man got into the jeep and piloted him to the filling station which had issued the receipt he had found in Kuzman Christoforov's pocket. There they went into the tiny office and, giving the number of the receipt, asked the man in charge to look and see when it was issued. The petrol had been bought round about 1.15 a.m. of the day in question.

This was not the answer he had expected and he insisted on

the books being checked, but there was no doubt. The person in charge had not come on duty until midnight. He remembered not being called on to give anyone petrol until after one o'clock and Christoforov's receipt was only the second one of the day. If he did not get his petrol until 1.15 in the morning, he could not have got back to Momchilovo before four o'clock at the earliest, that is to say, nearly two hours after the attack on the sentry at Iliazov's House, which seemed to indicate, in fact to prove, that he was not the author of that crime as Zakhov had been on the point of believing. If that was the case, what was the significance of the blue gloves? Could there be two pairs? He felt that he must sit somewhere quietly and think. Near the police station he had seen a barber's, so, driving back to it, he asked the plain-clothes man to wait in the jeep, went inside and asked for a haircut and no conversation, emphasizing the word *no*. The barber worked away in silence, then just as he was about to trim his dumb customer's sideboards with a razor, the man's face lit up, he jumped up abruptly, thrust a few coins into the astonished barber's hand and strode out.

Zakhov knew which hotel Boyan Icherenski usually patronized during his weekends in Plovdiv, but he had a hunch that he would find him registered at a different hotel for the night of 22 August. He and the policeman now began a search of the good second-class hotels which were not too expensive, and after drawing blank three times they found what they were looking for at the Hotel Trimontium in the older part of the town. Asking the manager to let them see the registration cards of all visitors who had stayed in the hotel on the night of 22 August, they found it: *Room 270—Boyan Icherenski. Passport 23851H. Departure during the night of 22–3 August. Time unspecified.*

Boyan Icherenski, but the writing and the signature were in the hand of Kuzman Christoforov. There could be no mistaking those large, rounded letters. Now, the pieces were beginning to fall into place.

Back at the police station, Zakhov rang up Sofia and had a brief conversation with Colonel Manov, whom he asked to arrange for the two soldiers attached to the Geological Survey at Momchilovo to be replaced by two others who would have orders to admit Zakhov at any hour of the day or night and not to reveal their instructions to the Survey.

For the third time the jeep with Zakhov and his plainclothes guide drove off from the police station. This time they had not far to go. The address was that of a house in one of the small streets at the back of the municipal theatre. It was one of those houses built before the First World War, two-storeyed with sun-blinds over the windows and consoles under the two little balconies outside the upstairs windows. The door was opened by an elderly woman in a dark dress. Her face was thin and lined, but delicately featured, and obviously she had been good-looking if not lovely in her youth.

'Madame Icherenska?' she said in reply to his query. 'I'll see if she's in. Who shall I say?'

'A colleague of her husband's,' Zakhov said, smiling his most winning smile.

He was ushered into a small hall, with walls panelled in some red wood, and a ceiling of the ornamental plasterwork that the well-to-do affected in the distant days when the house was built. It was remarkable that it had survived. There were one or two old pieces of furniture looking rather neglected; neither they nor the floor were as clean as they should have been.

'I am Madame Icherenska's aunt,' the woman said. 'We let out the ground floor and ourselves live upstairs, on the floor above.' She pointed to a spiral flight of stairs, with a polished balustrade and treads of the same red wood as the panelling in the hall, and, beckoning him to follow, led the way up. The stair-carpet was threadbare and faded, but the treads were broad and possessed a certain dignity.

The woman ushered Zakhov into a little drawing-room and asked him to be seated, while she went to see if her niece was in.

On a table was an old-fashioned photograph album. Idly he picked it up and began flicking through the pages. Suddenly his attention was caught. This man elegantly dressed in the style of the twenties was—Boyan Icherenski! But he could not be. Underneath was written: *Stefan, on the day of his second wedding.* Stefan? Stefan Stratev. So like Boyan he could have been his father.

And, according to the reports from Sofia, Illary Stratev and Boyan Icherenski had attended the same Institute of Mines and Technology. They must have known each other: both of an age, both Bulgarians living abroad. Of course, they must! One had returned. What about the other?

He heard steps outside and put the album down. The aunt came in and told him that Madame Icherenska was in and would come to see him as soon as she was presentable.

Zakhov looked round the drawing-room while he chatted with the aunt. It was crammed with furniture, most of it cluttered with photographs, vases and similar bric-à-brac, which made him wonder whether the children—if the Icherenskis had any children—were ever allowed in there. It was certainly no place for inquisitive fingers. There was one little stool covered with really lovely needlework, worn and faded, but still enchanting, that he particularly liked.

At the end of ten minutes or so, Madame Icherenska came in. She was tall, slim and looked about thirty. Her hair was obviously peroxided; her lips were rather thick and freshly made-up. It was a handsome face with a surprisingly white skin. There was a tired look about her eyes, as though sleep and she were scarcely on speaking terms. She was wearing a coffee-coloured dress with a gold brooch at the point of its V-neck. She held out her hand and Zakhov kissed it with the old-world elegance and courtesy that he affected.

'Your husband asked me to bring you his greetings and tell you how much he regrets it, but duty will prevent him coming to see you this week-end,' he said, pulling up a cane chair beside her and sitting down.

'I see,' she said and the utter indifference in her voice came as quite a shock. 'What a pity,' she added, but there was no warmth or emotion in her voice.

He produced his cigarette case and proffered it. She took a cigarette and, as she held it for him to light, he noticed that her fingers were stained with nicotine. She never asked about her husband or why he couldn't come; she just smoked in silence, obviously intending to leave conversation to him.

'Our geologists have been sent off on some urgent ploy and are now somewhere among the mountains,' he went on, trying to appear animated and gay. 'I'm in Momchilovo on a mission too, but a very different one. I'm an archaeologist delving into the ancient history of the region. It's an interesting place, but I expect you've been to Momchilovo so often you know all about it?'

He paused and she looked round at him.

'Not I,' she said, 'I've only once been in the beastly place.' She blew out a cloud of smoke, and added, 'And I hope I shall never have to go again.'

'You'll be the loser if you don't go,' Zakhov said. 'You must have heard the name of Momchil at school. The place is called after him, because it was where he won his most resounding victory. The actual capital of his kingdom was farther to the south, but Karabair was his fortress and I'm hoping—but I see I'm boring you, you don't like history or mountains, I do believe.'

'Neither, I'm afraid,' she said with an expressionless face

that certainly did not invite further talk. There was a long pause.

'At least you ought to cultivate a love of nature in your children,' he said with a smile.

'I have no children,' she said in a quiet voice.

'Comrade Victoria Strateva,' Zakhov said in a slightly pompous tone of voice. 'God is good, so are our doctors. You are young and I am sure you will have lots of children, if you want them.'

She gave a little shiver, as though she had glimpsed another frightening prospect. But she did not say anything. There was another pause, then he got to his feet.

'Have you any message for your husband? Not that I shall be seeing him for the next day or so.'

'None, thank you,' she said and held out her hand, which he again kissed.

Returning to the police station he sent an urgent message to Sofia requesting photographs of Boyan Icherenski as a youth and of his parents.

It was almost evening when Zakhov left Plovdiv on his way back to Smolyan, where he picked up a driver to take the jeep back after dropping him at Momchilovo. He sent the jeep along at a good pace, driving with the confident bravado of a man who feels on top of the world, for whom everything is going well.

18

THE RAIN came on just after he had left Smolyan, and although the jeep had a hood, its sides were open and the wind had kept flinging scurries of rain at its two occupants, so that by the time he reached Momchilovo Zakhov was saturated to the bone. He decided to put his head in and see if Anna had lit a fire.

The door opened the moment he had knocked, almost as if she had been waiting for him. Her face was gay and smiling.

'Gracious, you're soaked,' she exclaimed when she saw the state of his clothes. 'Come to the fire and get dry.'

Gratefully, he walked across to the hearth, where the fire was blazing.

'Now then,' she said, 'off with that jacket,' and she hung it upon a wooden peg where it began steaming almost at once. 'Now those,' she said pointing to his trousers, the legs of which were dark and sodden. She produced a wonderful old embroidered coat that had been her late husband's when he was a young man. It was more a work of art than a garment. Looking down at himself, Zakhov said, 'I ought to be doing a folk dance —but I'm far too hungry. I must get to Ilcho's.'

'No need for that. I have ham, eggs and peppers all waiting for me to cook them.'

'I can't wait,' he said.

Anna asked him what he had been doing all day.

'Roaming about,' he said. 'Searching for ancient sites and things. I'm an archaeologist, as you know. That's what interests me.'

'You don't need to go far for antiquities,' she said. 'You've got one here.'

'I don't think you're ready for carbon-dating yet,' he said. 'Other dating, yes; but not that.'

They laughed.

'Now you go and sit down,' she said, 'while I cook.'

The sky was overcast and it was still raining when he left the house just before midnight. He had spent a more than pleasant evening and, reluctant as he was to stick his nose outside, he had a lot still to do: two houses to break into, in fact.

He walked along as fast as the thick, rather slippery mud allowed him, in order to retain the pleasant warmth in his body. Once he put his hands up to his face and smiled to himself.

The air felt raw and cold on his face. It took him nearly half an hour to reach Iliazov's House. He paused by the small side door and wondered whether he should not have made sure that the old guards had been replaced before paying this visit. He coughed and opened the door. Out of the darkness, a voice he did not recognize said, 'Who goes there?'

'I want to check my watch,' he said. 'What time is it?'

'Pass,' said the voice.

He walked into the courtyard and made his way across to the main door of the house. He felt that he ought not to be seen picking the lock and decided not to use his torch. This was an unwelcome handicap and it took quite a struggle to get the heavy door open. As he had expected, the lock on the storeroom door was child's play to pick and he was inside within a minute. His first act was to drape his jacket over the narrow window; then he switched on his torch, made sure that the window was properly covered, then went to the door and switched on the light.

The centre of the room was occupied by a heap of surveying

instruments: tripods and levels, sextants, tape-measures, plumbs, drawing instruments, bottles of Indian ink and books of mathematical tables. Opposite the window were shelves, and on the middle one he saw a number of envelope files. He picked up the biggest and found it to contain what he had hoped: the Survey's journal and day book. With these he retreated to a corner, sat down with his back to the wall and began to read.

At first he flicked through the pages until he came to the beginning of August, when he gave the entries all his attention. There it was: on 10 August the geologists under Captain Kaludiev had made a fourth reconnaissance of an area to the south-east of Karabair; the co-ordinates of the north, south, east and west limits of this operation were given, as well as those of various other points. The eastern co-ordinates agreed to within a few tenths of a degree with those given by the monitoring service for the place of transmission of the clandestine ultra-short message that they had intercepted and—he remembered—still not decoded.

Involuntarily his hand went to his pocket in search of a cigarette, but then it struck him that he ought not to smoke, and he withdrew it again, empty. Next in the file was a sketch map giving the route taken by the group and this showed that they had returned from the most easterly point of the trip almost direct, their route taking them north-north-west through a deep, narrow valley that abutted on the road between Lakité and Momchilovo.

On 19 and 20 August the group had been in the field again and set off for home from approximately the same position. Thus it seemed that there could be no doubt that the person sending the messages was a member of the Geological Survey. He put the papers back in the file and restored it to its place. How, he wondered, had the spy got the necessary privacy to make his transmission. Granted he could have had the transmitter cached near by, but he needed at least fifteen minutes alone. Had he lagged behind and hoped nobody would come back to see if he was all right, or had he gone behind a bush, telling them to go on and that he would catch them up when he was ready? The time had been in the evening, so presumably there had been a moon. A glimpse at the calendar confirmed that there had been. There would thus have been nothing extraordinary in this procedure, and it was a technique that could be used, once, twice, perhaps, but surely his being taken short three times in the same place at the same time must have struck some of them as curious, yet nobody had mentioned it. Or was he the sort of person who was always having to dive behind bushes? Anyway, Zakhov had learned all he needed to know, so he took one last look round to see that everything was as he had found it, switched off the light, took his jacket from the window, put it on again and left the room. The lock clicked obediently into place behind him.

When he left the shelter of the courtyard of Iliazov's House, he found that the wind had got up and the rain become much heavier. The house he intended to break into now was the fifth along the Lakité road after Ilcho's tavern, so he had quite a walk ahead of him in the pouring rain, but he was too elated with his discoveries to mind. According to Marco Krumov, the taverner, the owners of the house had moved to Madara, where the husband had found a new job, several months before, thus Icherenski was living there alone, and there should be no one in the house when he got there. The house was surrounded by a high brick wall and Zakhov approached it without making any real attempt to lessen the sound of his footsteps or to hide himself from possible prying eyes.

The first thing that put him on his guard was a smell of petrol and hot rubber and metal; then, suddenly, there in front of him was a car. It was as though it had sprung out of the ground. He pulled up short. Although the smells had alerted his senses, his mind had not taken in the implication, and the realization that there was someone there came as a shock. Who? And above all why? The car was a jeep with the hood up, and appeared to be empty. He approached it warily. It was empty. The radiator was hot to the touch. He could not quite make out the number, but felt that he dared not use his torch, at least not yet.

Just beyond the jeep was a door in the brick wall. It was slightly open. He gave it a push and saw that it gave access to the courtyard, across which was the main door of the house. He slipped inside, half expecting to be hit on the head as he did so. He looked round for signs of the occupant of the jeep, then up at the upper storey. There! Behind one of the windows was a glow, you couldn't call it a light, but it was just the sort of glow you would get if there was somebody there using a torch. Treading very softly and cautiously he made his way across to the door that he could see as a black rectangle in the white-washed façade. It was shut. Slowly he turned the handle and applied a little pressure. It did not move. More pressure. As firm as a rock. He did not dare use his torch, but his searching fingers told him that it was a safety lock. He had no strip of celluloid on him—anyway, he had found that that system did not always work. He was not going to get in that way!

Stepping back from the door he looked up at the front of the house. There was only one way: the balcony that ran round the second storey, just under the roof. From his pocket he produced a grapnel and cord and, moving until he was beyond the end of the balcony, he wound his handkerchief round the hook to muffle the sound of its landing; then he swung his arm and threw. This was a thing that he had practised again and again, but it was so dark that his first throw was not hard enough and the grapnel fell back. He just caught it in time. The next throw was better, nicely judged in fact, and the grapnel flew in under the rail and fell with hardly a sound.

Though even that little thud brought his heart into his mouth and he stood rigid waiting, in case there was any reaction from the room with the lighted window. Nothing. Cautiously he pulled on the rope. The grapnel caught in the floor first time. Then, slipping off his shoes, he took hold of the cord and, bracing his feet against the wall, began to climb.

The effort of heaving himself up over the edge of the balcony without making much sound left him wanting to gasp and pant, but he had to control the urge. Rolling over, he lay still, one hand on the butt of the pistol in his pocket in case the other intruder had heard him and came to investigate. When his breathing was more or less normal again, he inched his way along until he was above the window in which the glow was. At that moment there was a click and the glow was replaced by bright light that sent a great shaft across the courtyard, lighting up the wall on the far side. Involuntarily he shrank away from the edge of the balcony, and it was a minute or more before he finally decided to lean over and see what was going on in the room underneath.

Inside, standing beside what looked like a plain kitchen table, was Victoria Icherenska. She had a scarf tied round her head and was wearing a green coat. The top of the table was littered with kitchen forks, spoons, knives and tin-openers. Then she pulled the drawer out farther so as to get at the things at the back and pulled out what looked like one of those old collapsible silver drinking cups. She then pulled up a chair and sat down, but in doing so she half turned her back to the window, so that after that he could not see properly what she was doing, but judging by the movements of her arm, she appeared to be polishing something, unlikely as that was.

After a while she paused, looked round, picked up a notebook lying on the table, tore a leaf out of it and after rummaging in a bag standing on the floor beside her chair, produced a pen and wrote two, perhaps three, lines on a piece of paper and slipped it between the leaves of a fat book lying on the table. It appeared to be a big recipe book.

All this had taken perhaps four or five minutes, as Zakhov saw when he withdrew his head to look at his watch. When he looked down again, she had removed her headscarf and was busy putting various articles off the table, including the silver drinking-cup, into it. Then she knotted the scarf and put it in the large leather bag on the floor, and began sweeping the other things back into the drawer in the table. He saw her push the drawer home, then her hand went out, there was a click and the room was plunged in darkness.

Realizing that he had only a few seconds to get out of the courtyard ahead of her, Zakhov leapt to the end where he had climbed up, swung himself over the edge and just let himself drop. He landed awkwardly with a nasty jar that sent a stab of pain up his thigh, but he had no time to worry about that; scuttling across the yard, he had just reached the door in the wall, when he heard the front door of the house opening. He froze. He saw the vague outline of a figure in the darker frame of the doorway and as she turned to close the house-door, he silently edged through the four-inch gap between the door and its jamb, and wondered where to hide. There was no cover that he could see; so he must either flatten himself against the wall and hope for the best, or hide under the jeep. Then he realized that he was on the wrong side of the jeep to flatten against the wall, because the jeep was pointing in his direction, so that the moment the headlights were switched on he would be mercilessly revealed. What would a woman in her situation do? Drive at him? Or let him arrest her, which he did not want to do—yet? He really had no choice. He could hear her footsteps as she crossed the courtyard. He tiptoed to the far side of the jeep and crawled underneath just as the footsteps reached the door. The door shut; then her feet appeared, rather unsuitably shod in high-heeled shoes, and the bottom part of her legs. She seemed to be stowing her bag and, judging by the sounds, was putting it on the floor between the front and back seats. Then one foot disappeared and the next moment she was in the driving seat. A grating whirr just above his head told him that she had pressed the starter, but the only response from the engine was a cough. She tried again: the engine fired once or twice then stopped again with a splutter. Once more she pressed the starter with the same result. Then her feet swung into view again; he heard a clank or two, then came the gurgle of liquid being poured and a strong smell of petrol. More clanks, then the feet vanished again, the starter whirred and as the engine sprang into life, he slithered out at the back, hoping desperately that she would not reverse as a preliminary to turning. Then she switched on the lights and the sudden brightness made him feel that she could not help seeing him; reaching up, he clasped his arms round the spare wheel and the next moment the jeep jerked forward. Clinging on grimly, he managed to get his feet braced against the mudguard; then, thrusting one hand over the back seat, he found that he could just reach the leather bag. Praying that she would not look round, he pulled. It yielded and, just as she changed up into second, he swung it up and over the back seat. Then, clasping the bag, he let go of the spare tyre and fell, trying to do a ju-jitsu roll as he landed.

For several seconds he lay clasping the bag and listening to the sound of the jeep's engine. Would it stop—and turn and come back? No, it went on. Once the note altered, as she changed into top, but after that it continued on the same note, just growing fainter and fainter, until he could no longer hear it. Then he got to his feet, dusty and feeling rather battered, but very pleased.

Walking back to the house, he found that his jemmy opened the door in the wall. He climbed up to the balcony again and, when he hung from it in front of the window in which the light had been, he found that he could just push this open. It was an easy matter then to swing himself inside. Then he saw that one of the panes was missing.

In the leather bag he had whatever it was she had gone to fetch, but he wanted to see what else was there and to get the piece of paper from the book. On this he read the somewhat cryptic message:

> Boyan—I have tidied up. You *must* be more careful with your things—V.

then he poked his nose into everything, as he considered the good sleuth ought to do. He noticed two bottles labelled 'Champagne Bulgare', both half-empty; there was a tiny red circle between the two words on the label of one. It gave off a sort of medicinal smell, certainly a smell of something that was not wine. The other bottle seemed to contain just rather flat 'champagne', but he decided to take it too in case analysis should show it to contain things not quite so innocent. Then he examined the window. The missing pane had obviously not been puttied in, but just nailed, and the nails had been carefully and neatly drawn, so that it almost looked as if the pane had been removed whole and for some definite purpose, which he was now beginning to glimpse.

He could find nothing else to interest him, so carefully lowering his bottles to the ground, he climbed down after them, shook his grapnel free and made for home.

It was almost five and beginning to grow light when he got to Anna Balabanova's house and tiptoed up the wooden staircase to his room. All at once he felt absolutely exhausted and realized that he hadn't the strength left to examine his finds properly. First he must have some sleep. The sun, he knew, would be round his side of the house about nine o'clock and that was bound to wake him; so that, unless the sky was heavily overcast, he would not sleep later than that. Kicking off his boots and removing his jacket, he sank down onto the bed, pulled the covers over him and was asleep within seconds.

19

SUNLIGHT and the sound of a voice singing woke him. He looked at his watch: it was 8.50—and a lovely morning. The singing continued and, getting up, he opened the door and went out onto the balcony.

Looking down he saw Anna Balabanova walking along underneath with an armful of firewood. She looked up, saw him, stopped singing and said, 'You're a late starter, I must say. Know what time it is?' He nodded, then she went on, 'I'm just off to the farm, but there's some coffee left. Would you like it?'

'It would save my life,' he said.

'Oh well, then, I can't have a death on my hands,' she said and disappeared round the corner of the house.

A minute later she reappeared carrying a tray on which were two steaming jugs and a large cup. He hurried down the stairs and took the tray from her.

'I'm off now,' she said, 'see you this evening.'

'Thank you for this,' he said and, turning, mounted the stairs.

With the coffee beside him, he began examining the trophies of the previous night. What intrigued him most was the drinking-cup. This was of silver, quite old and most beautifully chased. As he turned and twisted it in his hands examining it and looking for the hallmark, he felt a slight lateral movement that he thought should not have been there. He gave a gentle twist: the two top sections moved round a short way, but would go no further; then he saw that round the lip of each, in such a position that it would be hidden by the overlap even when the cup was pulled to its full height in the normal way, was a line of letters each in a square, thus:

Top section	C	A	R	M	I	N	E
Second section	D	U	M	T	A	L	I
Third section	S	I	L	V	A	S	A
Bottom section	N	I	M	O	S	Q	U

It was Latin, but beyond that he had no idea what it said. He also presumed that it did not matter, for this would be the code, the key to the messages. Then he noticed another thing: the letters themselves were painted or discoloured. Cupping his hands round one section and putting his face close to keep out the light, he saw that they were luminous. The code could be used in the dark.

Running downstairs, he made sure that the house was empty, then he produced his transmitter and began dictating the code to Sofia. He was just about to sign off at the end, when a thought struck him and he added: INSTRUCT POLICE PLOVDIV ARREST VICTORIA ICHERENSKA AND OWNER OF JEEP SHE USED LAST NIGHT.

At that moment he heard the sound of an approaching motorcycle. It stopped outside the house. Hurrying down he saw a dispatch rider holding a large envelope, a look of puzzlement on his face. Where could he find Mr Zakhov, he asked. Zakhov explained who he was, signed for the packet and the man mounted his motorcycle and rode off.

Returning upstairs to his room, Zakhov opened the packet

and found himself looking at a couple of family groups. *Christaki, Zenia and Boyan* was written under them. One was dated 1936, the other 1937. Who was this slight, rather intellectual-looking man with his small head, slight build, delicate hands? Could such a person have fathered Icherenski? Or this delicate little woman been his mother? He felt convinced that Boyan was not Boyan Icherenski at all, but Illary Stratev. What had happened to the real Boyan Icherenski? They had both been abroad in 1938, 1939. They had not got back before the war broke out, so presumably had spent those four or five years abroad. One had returned—but the other? Had the other not survived? Was this a case of a great impersonation?

By now it was too late for breakfast, but he decided to go to the tavern and throw himself on the mercy of Marco. He walked through the autumnal sunlight with a light step humming to himself Anna Balabanova's song. Marco served him a couple of eggs and, as he ate, they chatted. It was no difficult matter to turn the conversation on to the absent geologists and so to Icherenski's wife.

'If I was in his place,' Zakhov said, 'I wouldn't leave her in Plovdiv. Icherenski's got good quarters here and plenty of room, I believe, so what prevents them living together like everyone else?'

Marco just shrugged.

'Has she ever been to Momchilovo?' Zakhov asked.

'Oh, yes,' Marco said. 'Twice, I think, but only for a matter of hours. I don't believe she's ever spent the night here.'

As soon as he had finished, Zakhov went up to the Co-operative Farm, rang up Smolyan and asked for the jeep to be sent for him again, as he wanted a chemist to test the bottles of champagne and see if the one did contain a narcotic, as he imagined. At the police station in Smolyan he was told that Victoria Icherenska was already under arrest.

It did not take the laboratory long to confirm that the one bottle had had a fairly strong narcotic added to the wine, while the other was unadulterated 'champagne' which, though flat, was anything but noxious. With this information Zakhov set out for Momchilovo again, dismissing the jeep a mile from the village and going on from there on foot.

He was feeling rather hungry again when he reached Anna's house and hoped he might find her there, but the door was closed and locked. In his own room he did not have so much as a biscuit, but now he had not time to go to the tavern, as he was due to call up Sofia in less than an hour. He lay down on the bed and smoked to still the pangs of his rumbling, empty belly.

All the pieces of the jigsaw seemed about to fall into place and he now found the archaeologist in him coming uppermost and began wondering where Momchil's capital really had been. He tried to envisage the plain to the south of Karabair; the low, golden hills that rose out of it here and there, rather like the photograph he had seen of Kopjes in South Africa; the groves of olives and vines often gave a clue, because when people found that such things grew well, they left them there. Such sites could be thousands of years old. He decided he must ask for aerial photographs or get the department to borrow a plane for him so that he could fly over the area and look for the tell-tale signs himself.

As the time approached, he got out his set, put the headphones on and lay on the bed waiting for Sofia's call sign. There it was! He answered.

For the next hour he was busy taking down Sofia's messages, which included the full text of the three clandestine broadcasts which it had now been possible to decode, and how the code was used. He was also told what he already knew, that Victoria Icherenska and the owner of the jeep had both been arrested. He then asked for, and was given, the frequency on which the three clandestine transmissions had been made and acknowledged.

After this he got very busy: he went to Grozdan's house and found the old man just stretching himself awake after his siesta. Tucking his arm under the other man's, he led him out into the courtyard.

'Two things,' he said, 'and both rather important. The first concerns you as the local Party Secretary. I need four absolutely reliable men. At least, I don't need them myself, but I want two of the men to keep a close watch on Icherenski and the other two on Kuzman, from the moment the geologists return, and to make certain that they do not leave the village. If either tries, or looks as though he is preparing to try, I want to be informed at once. I shall be at Anna Balabanova's.

'Secondly, two police officers in civilian clothes will arrive later this evening. One is to be taken to Mrs Nadka's and given the use of a room looking on to the front of Anna Balabanova's; the other is to be taken to the Spiridon's and given a room adjacent to the vet's. Is that clear?'

The old man looked at him and nodded.

'Perfectly,' he said. 'Are you sure the geologists will return today?'

'Well, yes. They took only enough provisions to last two days from the tavern, so they'll get pretty hungry if they don't come back.'

Zakhov then paid another visit to the Farm and spoke to Smolyan on their phone arranging for the two police lieutenants to come in civilian clothes and report to old Grozdan. Briefly he explained what he thought they might have to do and gave them a few instructions.

It was about five o'clock when the geologists returned. Hungry and thirsty, as soon as they unloaded they hurried into the tavern, where Zakhov was just finishing his meal. They shook hands all round rather solemnly, then Zakhov, turning to Icherenski, said, 'I've made a great discovery. I think I've found the site of Momchil's capital.'

'But how splendid!' Icherenski said, a little coldly. 'Congratulations."

'Yes, it is exciting. To celebrate, I'll stand a special bottle of wine for our supper tomorrow.'

Getting up, Zakhov made room for the hungry newcomers at the table, took his leave and hurried back to his lodgings. As he was passing Mrs Nadka's house he saw a man lounging by the door smoking a cigarette. He had never seen the man before, but he appeared to be quite at home there. Zakhov looked at him, but did not speak; then the man took three quick puffs at his cigarette and Zakhov knew: this was one of the policemen and all was well.

The door of Anna's house was open and he could see her just inside. Smiling, she came out to meet him and he could not help feeling that she had been on the lookout for him.

Fearing an invitation, which on this night of all nights he could not accept, he decided to forestall her, so greeting her gaily, he said, 'Good evening; good evening. I've been on the go all day and I'm exhausted, but I think I've made a really great discovery. Now I must hurry upstairs and write a first report so that the lorry can take it to the post in Smolyan first thing tomorrow. But we must celebrate, so, if I may, I'll bring some bottles of Marco's wine tomorrow evening and you shall cook us something special and we'll celebrate together. Please say we can?'

Her face clouded momentarily with a shadow of disappointment, but then it brightened again and, looking up at him, she said:

'That's a bargain then. Tomorrow—I shall expect you about six.'

'I'll be there. I'm a very punctual person,' he said and with a quick movement he took her hand and kissed it; then he turned and hurried upstairs.

Locking the door, he got out his transmitter and began calling Sofia, using the emergency wavelength. Sofia answered at once and he gave his message: URGENT. ARRANGE FOR PLANE TO FLY OVER KARABAIR AT 2200 HOURS THIS EVENING.

The message acknowledged, he sat down at the table, got out the paper on which he had written the code, and began coding a message. When he had finished he looked at his watch; it was 9.25. Now he must just wait. He lit a cigarette and smoked it quickly and nervously; then lit another. At 9.45 he got out his transmitter and put it on the table with the coded message beside the key. At 9.55 he opened the windows and stood there listening. It was a clear, calm night and the few sounds of sheep in the distance and an occasional human noise travelled far. Somewhere a quail was calling. A sheep bell tinkled. Then he heard it—a distant hum that faded and swelled, but grew louder all the time. The plane! Quickly he turned, seated himself at the table and sat there, his hand on the key. When he judged the plane to be over Karabair itself, he began tapping out his message. And what a message!

URGENT FOR IMMEDIATE ACTION LIQUIDATE ARCHAEOLOGIST TONIGHT STOP GIVE SET AND CODE TO VET STOP NO FURTHER COMMUNICATION STOP YOUR WIFE WILL RECEIVE NEXT INSTRUCTIONS

He finished and sat listening to the plane, which had circled the mountain twice before flying off into the distance. The drumming on the roof of a sudden downpour drowned the last of the sound of its twin engines. Then the wind got up and the branches of the pine began tossing and swaying. He gave his head a shake. There was no time to stand there dreaming. He had things to do.

With a wry grimace at the thought of the pouring rain, he

took his raincoat and, rolling it up, stuffed it under the covers on the bed until it had the appearance of someone lying there, face to the wall. Then, leaving the window open, he stole out and downstairs and made his way to the woodshed. He knew that he would be invisible in the black shadow beneath its overhanging roof and there he seated himself in such a way as to have an uninterrupted view of the old pine tree and part of the balcony and settled down to wait.

Would his assassin come? Would he be Icherenski? Or was there a surprise in store for him? He felt inclined to bet on Icherenski—but there was always a but. His hand went to his pocket to confirm that he had his pistol. He waited.

It was not so much a noise as an awareness of movement that made him turn his head and see the indeterminate figure of a man making his way from the orchard to the old tree. Lithely the unknown—for he still couldn't see who it was—climbed the tree until he was standing on a branch so that his head and shoulders were above the level of the window-sill of Zakhov's room. Then he produced a dark object from under the breast of his coat. This object was in two parts which he seemed to be fitting together—a pistol, one of those which has a wooden holster that acts as a stock and butt. The pistol went to the man's shoulder, there was a brief pause, then in fairly quick succession three little 'phuts' and three tiny stabs of flame.

A silencer, he thought. In this wind no one else will have heard a thing.

The figure in the tree was now climbing down. It reached the bottom and turned and he saw the face: it was Icherenski.

Swiftly and silently the figure withdrew the way it had come. Zakhov gave it two minutes—longer he did not dare wait—then he too ran down the orchard, over the fence and made his way as fast as he could to the Spiridons' house.

He was quite out of breath as he reached it and, hoping the

old couple were heavy sleepers, he tapped on the young vet's window, paused and tapped again. He was just about to tap a third time, when the beam from an electric torch struck him and he heard the vet's startled voice saying, 'Who is it? What is it?'

'It's me, Zakhov. Let me in,' he called back.

A moment later, the door beside him opened and he slipped inside. The vet closed the door behind them and the two went into his room.

'Has the man from Smolyan come?' Zakhov asked.

'Yes. He's in the next room.'

'And the tape-recorder?'

'Is that the thing he put under my bed?'

'It will be. Now listen. You will shortly be receiving another visitor. When you hear footsteps, switch the recorder on. Like this. And leave it on. The person who comes in will be someone you know very well indeed. You must on no account show any surprise. You are to pretend to be expecting him and the parcel he will give you. Tell him that you have your own instructions about it and that he is not to worry. He will probably be in a hurry to go, so just let him. I shall attend to the rest. I shall leave you now, but I shan't be far away. I don't think you will have a very long wait.'

'I hope not,' said the vet. 'This cloak-and-dagger stuff isn't my line.'

The door opened and shut and thereafter there was silence. The vet stood for a moment, then decided that he had better get back into bed, that would look more natural. Then he remembered that he was supposed to be expecting his visitor, so he got up again and switched on the light. After that he just sat at the table waiting and growing more and more nervous.

At last he heard the sound of cautious footsteps in the courtyard and, bending down, switched on the tape-recorder. A moment later there was a soft bump against the outer door, as if someone had rested a heavy object he was carrying against it to free a hand. Then he heard a click of the latch and, getting up, opened the door of his room. The light that flooded out fell on Boyan Icherenski.

'Put out that light,' Icherenski said, and obediently putting up his hand the vet turned the switch and the room was plunged into darkness. For a moment they stood thus until their eyes had adjusted themselves, then Icherenski moved forward and put the heavy object he was carrying on the table.

'Here it is,' he said. 'Do you know what to do with it?'

'Yes,' said the poor vet in a voice choked with fear and nervousness. He would rather have said nothing, but he realized that in the gloom a nod would scarcely be enough.

There was just enough light to distinguish outlines, but little more.

'Right,' said the other. 'I'm off. I only wish they had told me to get out. I never suspected that you were one of us. Been in it long?'

'Not very,' said the vet. 'Good luck.'

'Thanks,' said Icherenski. 'I may need it.' Then he turned and made for the door.

He paused for a second in the extra blackness of the corridor, then there was a thud and a slithering sound. The door from the next room down the passage opened and the beam of a powerful torch showed Zakhov, holding a pistol by the barrel, bending over the figure of Icherenski, who was supporting himself with both hands on the floor and shaking his head.

'Let's tie him up,' Zakhov said to the policeman, who had come from the other room, and while they set to work, they could hear the shrill, quavering voice of old Mrs Spiridon from the back quarters urging her husband to go and see what was happening. A moment or two later the old man appeared, shirt hastily stuffed into a pair of trousers, which he held up with one hand. His eyes grew very round when he saw what was going on. The policeman straightened up and went to him, showed him his identity card, whispered a few words to him and, taking him by the shoulders, turned him round and gently urged him back towards his own part of the house, from which there came a mumble of voices and finally silence.

The two men then yanked Icherenski to his feet and pushed him into the vet's room, where they shoved him in a corner. There he sat gazing at the young vet, first incredulously, then with a look of venomous hatred. Meanwhile Zakhov was stripping the wrappings off the big parcel on the table, revealing a radio set which he examined with considerable interest. Then he turned to Icherenski and said, 'A good set, Comrade, but rather old-fashioned, isn't it?'

Icherenski looked at him; then he said, 'What is?'

'Your set, Comrade,' Zakhov said patting the object in question. 'This.'

'Never seen it before,' Icherenski said.

'It's not yours then?' Zakhov said.

'No, indeed.'

'Nor this either, I suppose,' and putting out his hand Zakhov jerked the big pistol from under the man's belt.

'No. I've never seen it before,' Icherenski said, giving Zakhov an insolent, contemptuous look.

'Indeed! Even though your fingerprints are on it and about half an hour ago you used it to fire three shots into my raincoat thinking it was me?'

'You're just being silly,' Icherenski said.

'And you didn't bring that here?' Zakhov asked pointing to the radio on the table.

'How could I, when I haven't seen it before?'

Zakhov walked to the other side of the room, knelt down

by the bed and thrusting his arm underneath it, pulled out the tape-recorder. Having wound it back, he set it working.

First there was a click, then the sound of a door opening; then Icherenski's voice said, 'Put out that light!' then a click, steps, a slight slither and a bump, then Icherenski's voice again: 'Here it is. Do you know what to do with it?' Then a hoarse, choking 'Yes' that it was difficult to recognize as the young vet's voice.

A click, and the machine was silent.

Zakhov pulled up a chair close to Icherenski and, sitting down, leaned forward so that his face was only a couple of feet from the geologist's. Lighting a cigarette, he smoked in silence for a moment or two, then he turned to the vet.

'Would your establishment run to some coffee?' he asked.

The vet nodded and produced a spirit lamp and kettle. Then Zakhov turned back to the other man and said:

'Now Comrade Illary, if you'll permit me to use your proper name. While we wait for our coffee, for I'm sure our young host will make some for you too, let me tell you a story, your story in fact, and you shall tell me if I go wrong anywhere.

'Quite a long time ago, there was a man in Plovdiv called Stefan Stratev who was agent for a number of foreign manufacturers of agricultural implements. He was happily married and had a baby son called Illary. When this Illary was four years old, that is in 1922, his mother fell head over heels in love with a foreign diplomat who came to take charge of his country's consulate, while the consul was on holiday. It was a grand passion for them both, and when the diplomat had to go back to his own country, Mrs Stratev threw all discretion to the winds and went with him, taking her young son with her. For a while they all lived together in the foreign capital, but then the diplomat decided to marry a young girl of his own country, who was something of an heiress. This he did, leaving Mrs Stratev in the lurch. She and her young son could not return home, as in the meantime Stefan Stratev had obtained a divorce and remarried, so they continued where they were, living under an assumed name. Then, fortunately for her, your mother then met an emigre Bulgarian who married her and looked after her and her son. Young Illary thus lived in a Bulgarian family, speaking Bulgarian, and learned the language of the country which, of course, was that used at the school he attended. He did well and obtained a bursary for foreign students given by the Adventist Church. Later, the Adventists sent him to study geology at the Institute of Mines and Technology, thinking this would make a good career for him. As a hobby young Illary studied wireless telegraphy, codes and ciphers.

'In this foreign capital there was at the same time another young Bulgarian called Boyan Icherenski. Boyan was the son of an emigre from Thrace, Christaki Icherenski, a merchant dealing in olive oil and Mediterranean fruits. He was a widower and his own parents were dead. In 1938 Christaki sent his son abroad to widen his horizons and complete his education and he entered the Polytechnic in the city where Illary was studying geology. The two may or may not have known each other—did they?' No answer. 'Probably they did. During the war Boyan was killed, probably in an air raid. He was not blown to pieces, but killed by blast. His papers and documents were handed over to the authorities. A year later his father, Christaki, died. Then when, in 1946, Illary, who had been recruited by his foster-country's Intelligence and provided with the other's papers, arrived in Bulgaria calling himself Boyan Icherenski, there were no relatives of the real Boyan Icherenski left alive who could have said that the present one was an imposter.

'As Boyan Icherenski, the young geologist and foreign agent possessed an anonymity and freedom of action that a member of the rich and numerous Stratev family could never have enjoyed. Perhaps he did not even know that his true name was

Stratev and that his real father had died two years previously, at the end of 1944, by which time he was once more a widower.

'It was not long before his duties brought Illary to Plovdiv, where he chanced to meet Victoria Strateva, his half-sister, though I don't believe he knew it. She was then living with her aunt. The two fell in love and married. When the physical resemblance between him and his wife's father struck them, only you can tell us. The realization of their true relationship must have killed at least her love, but by then she had already done so much intelligence work for a foreign power that her life was forfeit and you blackmailed her into keeping quiet about your true relationship and your activities as a spy. You are, of course, a clever geologist and in this respect have served your country well, discovering oil in two places, though at the same time sending your masters intelligence reports about it.

'At the beginning of April this year, you came to Momchilovo as a member of the Geological Survey. You became great friends with the local schoolmaster, Metodi Parashkevov, who had an amateur's interest in your own subject, geology. As your friendship grew, the schoolmaster confided to you that he had, or was pretty sure that he had, discovered a vein or deposit of leninite, vital in the manufacture of fissionable matter. He produced a sample and you, as a trained geologist, saw at once that in all probability the schoolmaster was right. The discovery so near the frontier of this metal was one of tremendous interest to quite a number of countries, and you reported it at once to your superiors. This gave rise to the exchange of a series of coded messages and various flights by high-flying reconnaissance craft, which first attracted the attention of our intelligence people.

'So far you had not managed to get an actual sample of the mineral, but you had learned the whereabouts of the deposit and wirelessed the map reference to your people. More, however, was needed and on the night of 20 August, you humped a transmitter to the area of the deposit, linked a radiometer to it and started transmitting the sound signals of the radiation from the deposit. This confirmed the enormous strategic and pecuniary value of the find and your superiors ordered you to make sure that the discovery was not made known. But how were you to prevent the schoolmaster, who had made the discovery, from telling his own authorities about it?

'You could never have got away with murder, nor had you any intention of putting your own neck in a noose by committing one. You devised a scheme whereby you could be pretty sure of the schoolmaster being executed by the very authorities who would have gained most by keeping him alive. It was an ingenious idea.

'I believe you must have been very slow in waking up to the fact that you were going to need gloves and did not possess a pair. When you did, you had to borrow a pair from Kuzman on some pretext or other. This was a pair Marie had knitted for him using some wool she had been keeping for herself and which was all she had.

'Sometime before this you had introduced Kuzman to your wife Victoria and the two had fallen in love, violently, as your own mother had done with her foreign diplomat. You had also, I imagine, told Kuzman that when you went to Plovdiv for the weekend, it was not to spend the night with Victoria but with another girl there, whose acquaintance you had made. Thus, when you brought Kuzman a note from your wife suggesting·a rendezvous for that Sunday night, he was only too keen to fall in with your plan. He knew which hotel you yourself stayed at and so went to another one, the Trimontium, but he signed the register in your name so that she might come to him.

'On the Friday night you had invited the schoolmaster to your place and given him wine, which you had drugged. The poor chap went to sleep at your table and you then pressed his fingers onto a pane of glass, the size of those in the window of the Survey's storeroom at Iliazov's House. When the poor man woke, he was muzzy-headed and very apologetic and hurried off home, feeling that he had made a fool of himself.

'On the Saturday afternoon you left Momchilovo on your motorcycle as though going to Plovdiv as usual, but you only went a few miles outside the village, hid your motorcycle and returned on foot once it was dark.

'You knew that Metodi Parashkevov had dinner with Marie, the game-warden's widow, every Saturday night and that he would come back very late and take the short cut that involved jumping the wall into the courtyard of Iliazov's House. It was a dark, stormy night and you had no difficulty in going to Anna Balabanova's house by the back way and climbing in through the window of the schoolmaster's room and stealing his towel. With this and a bottle of chloroform that Victoria had got for you in Plovdiv, you went to Iliazov's House just as the two soldiers were indoors handing over for the night watch, climbed the old tree in the courtyard and hid there.

'You must have had quite a wait and I only hope you were uncomfortable. Anyway, at last the schoolmaster appeared, stopped for a moment to talk to the sentry, then walked on. As the sentry was feeling for a cigarette, you dropped to the ground behind him, and hit him over the head. You then had several hours in which to stage the break-in of the storeroom about which we all know. After this you went back to where you had hidden your motorcycle and came riding in, ostensibly from Plovdiv where Kuzman had involuntarily given you a splendid alibi, late on Monday morning.

'Have I made any mistakes?' he said.

Icherenski looked up at him. There was a beaten look about him that almost made one feel sorry for him. Then in the distance they heard the hum of an engine: car or aeroplane? Car.

The policeman got to his feet as the car came to a stop outside. He turned to Icherenski and said, 'Time we were going'.

Obediently, Icherenski struggled to his feet.

20

AVAKUM ZAKHOV was a man of his word and that evening at six o'clock he walked up to the door of Anna Balabanova's house, his right shoulder distinctly lower than the left due to the weight of the basket he carried in his right hand.

Anna's eyes were dancing as she let him in. She was wearing a beautifully embroidered skirt and a blouse of the finest, rather transparent lawn cut considerably lower than he could remember having seen before in peasant costume. There was a great fire blazing in the hearth and the table was covered with a clean cloth and laid for two. From the kitchen at the back came the most glorious spicy smell to which he could not put a name. Setting down his basket, he looked at her. His face was quite serious as he gazed deeply into her eyes, then he smiled and taking a step forward, took her in his arms.

When they unpacked the basket it yielded two bottles of Marco's oldest and best, a bottle of plum brandy and a bottle of anis.

'Are you intending to make me drunk?' she said.

'Something of the kind. But we're both pretty intoxicated already,' he added with a smile. 'And I'm hungry.'

Later, as they sat beside the hearth, full, happy and relaxed, he said, 'I shall have to go to Sofia to report on my discovery tomorrow. Then I can take my leave. I have a whole month due to me. I had been going to the Black Sea. Would you like to go there?'

She stirred in his arms and looked up at him:

'The Black Sea?' she said. 'No thank you. I can't leave my sheep and my hills. I belong here.'

'Then I'll spend my leave in Momchilovo,' he said. 'There's a lot to discover here.'